I0667768

Mama ChaCha's School for Girls

(Or What Every Queer Boy Should Know)

Andrew Heller

ISBN 978-1-62806-321-9 (print | paperback)

Library of Congress Control Number 2021910158

Published by Salt Water Media
29 Broad Street, Suite 104
Berlin, MD 21811
www.saltwatermedia.com

Cover images by Camilla Morrison; design by Salt Water Media; editing by Mary Lib Morgan of Perfectly Penned; and author photo by Kelly Russo.

Mama ChaCha's School for Girls

(Or What Every Queer Boy Should Know)

For Paul: Mama ChaCha, Mother Cole, Auntie Pauline ... you were, are, so much to so many. Thank you. I love you!

For every queer young person who struggled, who will struggle, who is struggling: it is tough, but you are not alone and you are so enough! Please remember how absolutely worth it you are ...

For Ms. P: Paul Wegman, a brilliant talent, who helped shape and mentor my understanding and belief of theatre, expression, and the artistry within us all.

And for Wallace Eugene: you little piggopotamos. Yeah, you helped too ...

Resources

The Trevor Project
(866) 488 7386
www.thetrevorproject.org

LGBT National Youth Hotline
(800) 246 7743
www.glbthotline.org

LGBT National Hotline
(888) 843 4564
www.glbthotline.org

True Colors United
(212) 461 4401
www.truecolorsunited.org

PFLAG National
(202) 467 8180
www.pflag.org

PFLAG Salisbury
www.salisburypflag.com

"Yass girl! There is a tequila sunrise with your name on it!

♛

Vicky Fischer

Acknowledgements

Mama ChaCha's School For Girls (Or What Every Queer Boy Should Know) did not happen in a vacuum. There are so many folks who provided all sorts of support in different ways, and now is the time to say thank you:

First and foremost I must thank all of the drag queens who took the time to talk, chat, message, sit for an interview, converse, laugh, maybe share a drink or two with me. All added depth, experience, and fun. Vicky Fischer, you are a super star, a shining light, and a supreme talent. Fheanix Fischer (Allen Hickman), you are a fierce queen with a huge heart. I thank you also for keeping alive the legacy of your drag mother, Shaniqua Fischer. Anna Rexia Lords, you are simply fabulous! I could watch you perform again and again and again. Stormy Vain, thank you for the laughter and the real words of wisdom. And of course there is Missy ... she doesn't get out like she used to, but she's still got it.

I also need to thank Tony Russo and his storytelling event, One True Thing. You make me a better writer, Tony. Mark Delancey and PFLAG, thank you for lending your experience, name, and your trust to this project. Mary Lib Morgan of Perfectly Penned, I am so glad we stumbled upon one another because it was pure joy! And of course, the fine and fabulous folk at Salt Water Media: Steph ("The New Girl") and Patty ("Mrs. Heller") — y'all are family!

There are a few folks from my "Once Upon a Time" who offered clarity, assurance, and a lot of love. Bunny, I've been re-watching *Three's Company* and I thought you should know. Maggie May, thank you for the assurance, the understanding, and the memories. Kenny Preuss: y'all, he's a playwright! Skillet (Jeff Smith), I will drink your coffee and read your books! Camilla Morrison, you have always understood my heart. Thank you for being a part of this. Husayn Frazier, you probably know me better than anybody else, so, you know…

And finally to a few folks who were very much a part of this as they are very much a part of Mama ChaCha's heart and mine. Tim Flynn and Anita Hurst Wright, it has been a journey. Thank you. Sam Heller: I can't believe I let my kid test read this! And of course, Mike Parker, I love you!

Table of Contents

"For us it was Paris Is Burning. *For the new kids, it's* Pose. *But if you know your history, everything being seen today is a remake of the originals."*

♛

Stormy Vain

Foreword

When Andrew asked me to write his foreword for him, I have to admit, I was a bit out of my element, but was terribly honored and humbled. I've known Andrew for almost six years and he was one of my first friends I met in the LGBTQ community after moving to the Eastern Shore. Like many of us "old queens," we built our relationship at the local watering hole. Somewhere between all the scotches or vodkas — I lost count — our friendship took root.

When I sat down with him to discuss this project, it was clear from the start that his vision and words needed to take seed and grow. If not only for me to restore my nostalgic roots in which I feel so grounded, but also for all the saplings out there who will never understand the storms we went through so they can grow.

Between reading all his works, posts, and meandering thoughts he continuously creates on a daily basis, it's clear he has captured something great with this work. And like our mothers schooling us on how to bake for the first time, you will walk away the wiser for reading this. Because it's not so much about the stories or even the words, it's about how you feel when you finish the last words, close that book, go to the kitchen and smell that fresh homemade strawberry pie cooling on the counter sitting right next to the whisky sour and floured apron. Now pass me a knife, a plate and get me another whiskey sour. I got some stories to tell you.

Mark DeLancey
Executive Director, Salisbury PFLAG
Retired Marine, Old Queen and still kickin'

"You know what's funnier than some dude in a dress?
Some asshole getting his ass kicked
by that same dude in a dress."

♔

Missy

Introduction

This collection of short stories was a true labor of love born out of grief. Andrew began working on this book not long after the loss of his friend, Paul Cole, or as you will come to know him, Mama ChaCha.

While these tales may be funny and irreverent and a bit bawdy at times, these stories are also tender and touching and full of the one thing every young LGBTQ truly needs: a sense of real belonging.

Coming out of the proverbial closet is a difficult thing to do. There is fear and anxiety. Worry over family acceptance. Finding community and lovers, both casual and lifelong. Heartache. Friendship. And above all, learning to accept and love ourselves.

Every single one of those elements is in these stories because Andrew has lived, felt, and survived each and every one of them. Real life is a school of sorts, full of choices and teachers and moments in which we come to understand the world around us and how we fit in. That's what this book aims for ... to be a reflection of all those experiences — the good, the bad, the ugly, and, yes, the beautiful, unabashed wild.

As I read these stories, I couldn't help but feel like this was Andrew's way of reaching out and saying, "Hey you. Yeah, it's hard and weird but it will get better and you'll be alright. We are here."

And that's the lesson of this collection.

Stephanie L. Fowler
Sophie Kerr Prize Winner
And a person lucky enough to be Andrew's friend

"If your wig flies off, keep moving, bitch.
The show must go on."

♛

Shaniqua Fischer

A Note From The Author

(Or The Famous Mama ChaCha Snatched a Wig Story)

*M*ama ChaCha always had a story. Always. And while sometimes it would begin with "Did I ever tell you?" (Normally she had.) or "Oooh Girl, remember that one time?" (I didn't, because I was never there.), usually she would just start by mentioning some random fact about some random person I had never heard of, ever, not in my whole life.

Or Mama would just begin her declarative statements with a pronoun: "She died, I guess," never letting on who *that* she might be, but that random style was just how Mama ChaCha—Paul—shared.

None of us really remembers when Paul received the moniker Mama ChaCha. One friend suggested it came from his days in Wilmington. He worked at a drag club there, though not as a drag queen—at least that's how I understood it. Another friend clearly remembers the first time they met. Paul wore a sweatshirt emblazoned with the words *Mama ChaCha*. So we all called him Mama ChaCha. Even my son, Sam, did until he got a little older and funnier and would sometimes call him "my Auntie Pauline." Mama loved that! I believe that randomness was Sam's favorite memory of Paul; the randomness of launching into a story assuming his audience had the backstory. "Oooh girl, remember that time?"; "She died, I guess."

My initial intention with this collection was to throw together some cute and kitschy little parables—lessons for this fabulous title, *Mama ChaCha'a School For Girls*. It was a title that needed a book. For years before we lost Paul, I joked with him about writing this hilarious guide for figuring out life while gay in a small town, because that is what this book was initially going to be. But, as often happens, life gets in the way. Things happen. And things don't happen. And this thing never did.

When Paul got sick, we revisited the idea of the book, he and I. Only with the real life scenario unfolding before us, cute and kitschy didn't quite cut it. I still wanted the subject to be life lessons for coming of age queers; that had always been my intent. But I felt a more serious vibe might be warranted now. I was also working on a piece, now included in this collection, for the storytelling event *One True Thing*. My friend Tony organized the event where an author would read a ten to fifteen minute, non-fiction essay about resolution or resolve. "The Girl Who Lived In the Cabin Behind Me" was the result. I read the story to Paul and to others and got some favorable feedback. And I worked and reworked and learned new things about my writing— and about me. The story was well received at *One True Thing*, and Paul was thrilled to hear about how the event went. "I'm proud of you, sweetheart," he said.

Paul died in February 2020, just a few weeks later.

I think one of the saddest things about losing someone is the forgetting. That may even be the saddest thing about death, whichever direction you are looking at it from...

asshole. My dead friend, Janet, would always add "asshole" to the end of any sentence that ended in a preposition. Hers or someone else's; it really didn't matter. I mention her in "The Girl Who Lived In the Cabin Behind Me," the story I read at *One True Thing* and to Paul. A jarring side note, I understand, but these random thoughts or memories juxtaposed with the stark realities of grief are important. Memories heal, memories clarify. And I have gone off on a tangent, as I am wont to do, but the point is this: We were playing cards one night—and I forgot. I forgot Paul's voice. It was just for a moment, but it hurt. And it struck me so hard.

With more earnest and purpose than before, once again I set out to complete my project. I researched things, both in a lazy internet way and by some more serious reading. I interviewed a few folks, I touched base with some old friends, I touched base with some new friends, and I kicked myself for not having grilled Mama for more stories. I spent those last weeks telling her my story, and now I just wanted to hear hers. I wanted to hear her stories in the voice I so longed to remember.

I wrote this collection in no particular order. I believe "A Park-and-Ride Isn't Always For Parking and Riding" may have been the first story I wrote, along with a theatrical and dreamy version of a prologue and epilogue that were eventually reworked into the final story of this collection, "In the Name." And, of course, the only non-fiction piece, "The Girl Who Lived In the Cabin Behind Me" which was actually a late and much-debated addition to this collection. The others came more slowly, but still with the same angst, purpose, and goal. I hope my intended purpose of sharing stories that illustrate life lessons is achieved. I hope lessons revealed by the memories, the experiences, the embellishments and even some fun little lies of so many folks who are just like me, or just like you, or just like Mama ChaCha help my readers. And while they are not as light and hilarious as they were initially intended, I'd like to think the rawness, the realness, and the vulnerability are balanced by a little fun and maybe just a little bit of "naughty," too.

Though I had clarity of purpose and intense earnestness, something was still missing—and that was Mama ChaCha. Her voice, the one I forgot.

I can't begin to capture who Mama ChaCha was—I can't. But I do have to tell you at least one story that just may give you a hint before you dive into the rest. One that is not embellished or made up, and is not an elaborated or a glorified version of her. It is simple and short. And hopefully you will hear it being told in her voice, because I sure do! Short, sharp, loud, scolding...and filled with love!

> "You remember that time I snatched that wig off that drag queen? I did. I was on the dance floor. And I just danced right up to her and...shwoop! I just snatched it. I snatched that bitch's wig—just snatched it. She was up there, thinkin' she was better'n everybody else. Well, I snatched it!"

Now listen, class is in session, bitch, so take a seat!

Lesson 1:

Family is a choice, being gay is not.
Just as a park-and-ride is not
always for parking and riding ...

1

"Being a mother to a group of gays is a huge responsibility, but more than that, it is a responsibility that we as older gays should do with great pride to make sure the younger generations are led to excellence. And to pick up where there biological family might drop off."

Anna Rexia Lords

"When I learned how to suck a dick, I learned how to fight 'cause some of them bitches is ignorant!"

Fheanix Fischer

A Park-and-Ride Isn't Always For Parking and Riding

*H*e had heard about it as an offhand joke, "You can always swing by the park-and-ride for a blowie ..." Those words resonated, replayed, and lingered in his mind countless times..And as he replayed those words, he thought of the countless times he had heard similar things uttered, or intimated, or somehow suggested, and he had never really caught on. Like the times the big kids would laugh and point knowingly as they passed *that place* while on some bus ride for some field trip or sporting event. Or the times his father would make a snide remark or insinuation toward one of his hunting buddies. Or the times at work it was the joke he just couldn't quite get. Nope, for our young friend just exactly what these words and jokes and whispers meant—he hadn't really understood.

"You can always swing by the park-and-ride for a blowie..."

He drove past that place nearly everyday. It was just off the highway that runs towards the beach—not too far from town, but far enough to be out of the way of any real and regular traffic. He was a local boy, our friend, not one of the college kids. No, he worked to make his way in the world. But he had plans; he sure did. He was going to get out—get away. He was not going to be stuck here in this small time rural Hell.

It was just a paved circle, really, with about thirty parking spaces. The local transit bus would pull through four times a day, picking up or dropping off folks who decided they would park, then ride to wherever they were going. Work, perhaps a day at the beach. Even a few crafty students used it to avoid paying for a parking sticker at the local university. These were the typical reasons for leaving one's car at the park-and-ride.

It was a shady spot, with large mature trees and even a few picnic tables—truly a park. Along one side was a stretch of trees, dense vegetation, and a little stream. Perhaps irrigation ditch is the better word as the entire area was farmland once upon a time. And if one were to look closely enough, one might see a trail or two leading into that dense vegetation toward the little stream. Along the other side was the highway leading to and from everywhere, offering those in the know a glimpse of who or what may be at the park-and-ride. The remaining sides of the square lot with the circular drive were a smaller road, a few houses dotting a simple street that led to the entrance of the park-and-ride, and finally another road that would take you on a serpentine route of neighborhoods and businesses and back into town. That final side was what remained of a rather large and old family farm—dismantled now, eventually to be sold off, piece by piece, generation by generation.

He pulled in one night. It was late. He had just gotten off work. He was a server at one of the local chain restaurants on the north side of town. It was one of two jobs; his other, helping out on his sister's family farm. Corn and soybeans and six chicken houses. He didn't want to be a farmer, although he felt no shame in it. His family had been in the growing industry for generations.

But he had other ideas. He played the piano at church, and sometimes the organ. He was better at the piano. He wanted to go to school; he had gone so far as to check out classes at the local community college. But writing wasn't his strong suit, and he often avoided such things. Things that not so much challenged him; rather, they lessened him—made him feel less than. They were, perhaps, silly and unnecessary insecurities.

But then, aren't most of them? Insecurities? Yet they are a major influence in our lives—shaping and informing, steering and guiding.

———◇———

It was a warning light that inspired him to take the right turn and pull into the park-and-ride. It was his coolant. He had a small leak. He kept a jug on the floorboard behind the seat of his black Ford Ranger, an early '90s model he had managed to save for with earnings from his grocery bagging days in high school. He was a junior then, and he paid cash. He was going to get it fixed one day; he just needed to save a little more.

He pulled in and made a slow loop around the circle, looking for a place to park and refill his radiator reservoir. There were a few vehicles parked on the circle near the picnic tables where a few men sat. He parked in one corner, away from the cars on the circle and several spaces from the newer model SUV that had backed into its spot. He sat parked for a moment and looked about the lot. The men at the picnic table had all stood; they were looking—watching—no. *Looking* was the better word. He could feel their eyes on him so he just sat in his truck for a moment, thinking he would allow all his anxieties and insecurities to guide his next steps.

But in the next minute, he slid out of his truck and stepped down from the running board; so much for his anxieties and insecurities. With a half-full jug of coolant in his hand, he strode toward the front of the truck while the eyes of those across the way were locked onto his every move. He could hear muffled talking; he didn't have to hear the words to know that they were about him. He popped the hood, opened the cap to his coolant reservoir, and poured the brilliantly unnatural chartreuse liquid inside.

"Car trouble?" A man's voice came from somewhere to his left.

He spun around. Amazingly, not a drop of the neon syrup from the blue jug was lost.

"Oh fuck...sorry. Didn't mean to startle ya."

"Oh, yeah...no, I'm sorry I jumped," he spit out, as everything he'd ever heard about this place, and the men who stopped here, and the things they got up to flashed through his nineteen-year-old mind. "Just adding a little coolant. I have a slow leak. I'm getting it taken care of soon."

The moon was but a sliver. And the lone working streetlight cast not nearly enough of its silvery protection. It was a moody Herb Ritts meets film noir scene as a tall broad shouldered man stood towering over a slender yet fit younger man, jug in hand, leaning back against an older model black Ford. The young man was dressed in black, slim fit pants. If one were to look closely, the grease and wear of a practiced server could be seen in the overworn fibers. His tight fitting white t-shirt told both the stories of a hot kitchen and a long shift, as well as years of physical labor on his sister's farm.

The young man turned with his jug lifted and leaned into the task of adding coolant to his truck; the taller, older gentleman stepped back for a long look. The older gentleman's left hand lifted from deep within the pocket of his well pressed slacks. His shirt sleeves were rolled to his elbows and the diamond in his wedding band shot a flash of reflected light. The young man's eyes caught the flash and followed that wedding band as the hand brushed across the older man's strong jaw, before working its way back home—a little too deep in the pocket of his slacks. He admired the "lift with your legs" form of this hot little farm boy's ass.

"Need any help?"

""I'm good. Thanks, though." The young man shut the hood with an awkward slam. *Was that a little too loud? What the fuck?* He turned and faced the man, alternately looking at his intensely staring eyes and following the man's subtly busy pocketed left hand.

They stared at one another for a moment too long, and then the young man moved to get back into his truck. The older man stepped back and smiled, his hands raised as if to say "No need to worry." He followed the young man to the driver side door of the black Ford Ranger.

The young man leaned in, setting the coolant on the floorboard behind his seat, then climbed in, adjusting himself as he settled back into the seat. The older man stood smiling, enjoying the view. It was just a hint of a smile, and his left hand found its way back down. This time without the constraints of a pocket.

He shut the door, our young man did, and he stared forward just a moment. *What the fuck was that?* He sat just breathing for a moment, hands in his lap; he couldn't help but notice the fullness. He started the car and looked to his left. He was still being watched. He rolled down the window as he saw the man approaching once more.

"You heading home from work?" the older man asked.

"Uh, yeah, um, I'm a server at, well, nevermind." *What the hell, dude?*

"You, uh, you got a light? Mine's dead, and my other one's back in my car."

He stretched his legs out and lifted his hips as he struggled to reach the lighter in his own left pocket. *Fucking slim fit.* The darkness and the shadows hid much of the obstacle at the bottom of his pocket. *Dig—again—finally!* He retrieved the cold, hard rectangle. The gentleman stepped closer, leaning inside the car for the light. Hands trembling, our young friend attempted to light the man's cigarette and fumbled. The man smiled and took the lighter.

"Thanks." The man stood back and cupped his hand to his face. A deep glow followed an orange flash.

Our young man could only stare ahead, eyes locked on the older man's left pocket. It also seemed to be rather full. The young man found his hand in his lap again. *Holy fuck ...* he may have whispered his astonishment.

The silvery glow of the wedding band was lost when it entered the shadows beyond the truck's open window. "I'm just returning your lighter. Is that okay?" the man said calmly, deeply, quietly—resting the lighter and his hand firmly on the young man's lap.

"Um...okay....Yeah. Sure." Quick breath; pounding heart.

Two hands on his lap still; one on his steering wheel. "Um, thanks. Yeah, no. I..., um.... I need to go. Sorry." He was already shifting out of his former position and into gear as the gentleman smiled, maybe even laughed, and stepped back.

"I'll catch you next time." The man shouted as the younger one rolled up his window and drove off. The small group at the picnic tables was still watching the show. A few may have applauded.

Our young hero turned back onto the highway; sweaty hands gripped the wheel; eyes wide and locked forward. *I am never doing that again.*

Never came around soon enough as his indicator light soon came on again. It was daylight this time, early afternoon. He had just finished a lunch shift and was cut early. He hated the lunch shift unless it was a double, because he never really made quite as much as he did during the dinner rush. But he did have the rest of the day, as he told his sister he would not be working the farm that day—and he was going to make the most of it.

Our young man pulled into the circular lot. There were a few vehicles, mostly unattended; their owners must have parked and ridden. Over near the picnic tables under a shade tree, a well-driven, light green Oldsmobile Delta 88 was parked. Someone was inside this one. The windows were down. The older gentleman in the car was reading the newspaper.

The young man chose a spot and parked well away

from the man in the Olds. He sat for just a moment, taking in his surroundings, checking in with his insecurities. He made sure he would have no surprises like last time; no men in SUVs needing their cigarettes lit were nearby. He stepped out of his truck, jug in hand. It was a warm day in early spring. The sun had been shining, and the temperature was a rather pleasant 66°. He thought how funny it was that 66° seemed so warm after a cold winter, yet felt like an arctic blast when it hit again in the fall. He set the blue jug of chartreuse neon on the hood of his truck; then he removed his white button down shirt—part of his uniform from the restaurant. He tossed his shirt back inside through the open window and stretched. His pale skin did not offer much contrast to the dingy white tank he wore, a wife beater as some folks called it. He picked up the jug again, opened the hood of his truck, and added some more coolant to the reservoir.

"Hey darlin'." A slow cruising blue sedan passed by. It pulled through to where the man in the Olds was parked, and stopped just in front of him.

Two guys got out of the car—a tall thin guy and a shorter, rounder man. They resembled some modern version of Laurel and Hardy, a reference that would be lost on the young hero of our story. The pair strode over to one of the picnic tables and sat, one at the table, the other on it. The man in the Olds put his paper down and started up a conversation with the two newcomers, out of earshot of the boy with the blue jug still in his hands. He watched the trio for a moment, our young man did, and thought about what happened that night a few weeks past. One of the men, the skinny one, raised an arm and waved, shouting something our young man could not or chose not to make out. He got back in his truck and drove around the circle, slowly, eyes forward, hands at 10 and 2. He did not look as he drove past the men. The two at the table now stood and watched appreciatively, while the older man in the Olds just waved a friendly enough wave.

The young man drove away, not quite as hurriedly as he did before, his eyes trained on the gentlemen who watched as he left the park-and-ride and pulled back onto the dual lane highway that would carry him toward home, or to the beach, or perhaps simply away.

And so it went, the next few times that *never again* came around; he pulled in, did his coolant thing, someone generally said something or approached him or just pulled up next to him, and he nervously left. Yet one day he did not. Leave, that is.

"Well hey there, son," the older man with the newspaper in the green Olds called out of his window.

Our young man closed the hood of his truck, wiped his brow with the bottom of his shirt, exposing not quite a six-pack, but a flat and toned belly that certainly caught the eye of the older gentleman in the Olds. (Everyone loves a good "happy trail.") The boy turned and looked at the man. He was alone. There were no other cars in the park-and-ride that Tuesday afternoon. The young man held his hand up and waved.

"You still havin' car trouble?" and something else the younger man couldn't catch. He was significantly older—middle-aged, a little bigger in the middle, thinning gray-brown hair, and a voice that had more of an effeminate drawl than his stature would suggest.

"I'm sorry?" Feeling safer, braver now that no one else was around, the younger man took a few steps toward the Olds and the gentleman inside.

"I've seen you pull in a few times, and you always do something under your hood." The man's tone was displeased yet friendly, dismissive yet welcoming. "I said I guess it's car trouble."

"It's a thing with my radiator and coolant reservoir," the younger man offered. "It isn't a big deal; just annoying."

"Oh. I didn't know."

"I've seen you here before," the younger man ventured.

"Oh, yes. I come here on my days off and read the paper... just to see what's going on, I guess." The man looked as dismissively welcoming as he had before. "You've heard about what happens here, haven't you. That's why you're here?"

"I...uh," the young man blushed. "I mean..."

"Oh don't worry. I won't tell."

"I've never done anything. I'm not..."

"Most of them aren't, son." The man smiled, his dark blue polo shirt offering a glimpse of where he may spend his days when at work. "Like that one over there. He's married."

The young man looked in the direction where the older gentleman had nodded. A well-dressed man in his forties stood outside his car, a Mercedes. *When did he get here?* It was a C-class, not the super high-end luxury vehicle of that line, but the entrance level—just enough to give one an ego boost without completely breaking the bank. He smoked a cigarette. His long sleeves were rolled up to his elbows. His crisp, fashionable shirt was paired with well-pressed khakis. He stared over at our young man while the man in the Olds nodded subtly with encouragement. The man in the khakis gave a nod as well, before walking toward the denser trees that lined the stream, irrigation ditch—or whatever one might want to call it. He looked over his shoulder at them as he gradually disappeared on a well hidden path.

"Go on," the gentleman in the Olds said. "Walk on back there. He's safe. I've talked to him a few times. Don't be so nervous. We all know what happens back there. Where else are we gonna go?"

He didn't really register much beyond the encouraging words of the older gentleman, but like a sailor to a siren's song, he walked by the picnic tables, across the grass, and down the same path the "C-Class" man trekked before him. The path turned left, then right around some trees and undergrowth, and right again, following the shallow stream of water that ran past the park-and-ride and through the farm field turned commercial property—at least that's how the large billboard advertised the sale. He came upon the man who was now facing the stream, hands before him.

Is he peeing?

C-Class turned toward our young friend, just enough for him to recognize that, yes, C-Class was peeing. The young man, red-faced and trembling, stepped forward. Undoing the front of his black trousers, he also prepared to relieve himself.

The two stood side by side after both streams ended. Yet they both stood as though their relief had not been fully achieved; that there was more to come. Our young man looked forward, still trembling, nervous, confused; the anticipation and excitement inarguably growing in his own hands. And then a third hand entered his vision. It was smooth, tanned, well manicured. A thin white line on one finger confirmed that a ring protected that bit of skin from tanning. That hand now reached to offer assistance to this desperately anticipating young man who just happened to be relieving himself back in this hidden corner of small town America. That hand had offered assistance in the past to other young men, desperately anticipating next moves or just coming to a certain awareness in this hidden spot. That hand belonged to a man who, on other days and at other times, wore a ring his wife had picked out with great joy less than a decade before. That hand belonged to a man who was as eager as the younger one. Yes, C-Class was eager, too.

When our young man stepped out of the woods some twenty minutes later, it was, for him, the longest walk of shame in the history of such walks. The park-and-ride was bustling with activity. The transit bus pulled through the lot. The skinnier guy from a few weeks ago was there at the picnic table, and the nice man in the green Olds was talking with him. Another one of those nondescript American made sedans was parked next to his own black Ford Ranger. Red-faced and still shaking, he ran the last few steps to his truck. The man waved, but our hero hurriedly pulled out of the park-and-ride and drove away. *I cannot do that again. Oh my God, I can't.*

He would have that same thought about a month later. And then a week after that. It was another full week later when he finally spoke to the gentleman with the newspaper in the green Olds. He pulled in, our young man did, and smiled when he saw the familiar sedan. *I'm gonna have to get his name sometime and thank him.* He got out of his truck and turned to reciprocate the wave he knew was coming. Only it didn't come. There was no wave today.

Forgetting the pretense of adding coolant, he walked over to the older man's car and peered through the open window. And there sat the man, mouth agape, his right arm resting across his chest. The seat was reclined nearly flat, and the paper lay trapped beneath his arm. He looked rather peaceful. *Oh my God, he's dead!*

"I'm not dead, God dammit!" the man suddenly barked, throwing the newspaper aside, eyes still closed, a slight smirk crossing his face. "But girl, if you had just seen the size of the one I had today. Shoo. You'd be tired, too."

Two seconds ago, the young man was sure the old man was dead. But, to his relief, he quickly realized the old guy was in on the park-and-ride activity that he was just coming to appreciate. The old guy did what he encouraged the younger one to do back in those woods, beyond the undergrowth, along that shallow stream.

"I-I-I didn't mean to bother you; I'm-I'm sorry."

"Oh, you're fine...sweetheart," the man assured him. "How are ya today?"

"I...um, I-I-I pulled in because...."

"Oh, honey, you're fine. No need to be embarrassed. Bless your heart." The man was sitting up now. "They call me Mama ChaCha. I'm just everyone's mother, I guess."

And they spoke—for quite a while, too. And Mama emparted her second, and perhaps greatest lesson to our young friend. As more cars came in and out, more men stopped and took walks, or stood by their cars and smoked, or even sat

15

on the picnic tables and just chatted. Our young hero chatted with several of the folks who pulled through the park-and-ride that day. Oh, this place was alive! It had a pulse. It even had politics, like a little community. And it was a community...a community of strangers and anonymity; a tight-knit group of folks who knew very little about each other except the cars they drove, the names they were assigned, and—on occasion—what gossip could be gleaned from the world outside of the park-and-ride.

Mama ChaCha introduced the young man to several folks that day:

There were Farmer Jeff and Black Jeff. One was a local farmer and one was, well, he was a black guy named Jeff. He worked in real estate.

There were Myrna (clearly not his real name) and Chad, the Laurel and Hardy duo; they were not a couple, but they were almost always together.

There was One-Leg Mary; Mike was his actual name. He really did have just one leg. He lost the other from a childhood disease of some sort. A bone infection.

There was One-Eyed Sally. He had a birthmark over one eye and an unusually enormous cock. It was one of those you couldn't really call a penis. No, it was larger than that. It was a COCK.

And there was a whole host of other folks, too. But this was the core group, the heart of the park-and-ride. For the most part, they hung out at the picnic table, smoking cigarettes, swapping war stories of conflict and climax back beyond the trees here or at some other locale with a similar dark secret, but also sharing problems of work, family, and home.

"Why don't we ever meet at a bar somewhere? Isn't there a bar or some other place we could all go hang out at?" Our young hero queried his friends one day.

"Where?" came one reply. "Where would we go? I haven't seen a gay bar here since, well, never."

"There was that one bar, but it got rough once folks figured out we were there," said another.

"It was never really a gay bar either, just a place we could go until it got weird," the skinny guy, Myrna, interjected.

"This isn't DC or Baltimore," Mama offered. "They don't have those here. They would never allow it."

<hr />

They would never allow it. That thought, those words, they stayed with our young hero as he finally went away for a few years. Our young man went to college. He started at the local community college but after several years of kind-of-sort-of-maybe part-time status, he transferred everything and went to school in the big city. Well, near one anyway. And a whole new world of liberal values and views opened up to him. For better or for worse, he could be open about who he was on campus. There were even groups and clubs he could join. With newfound friends his own age, he began making connections. There were bars he could go to, and people felt comfortable being who they were, right there in the open. He went dancing, and he saw his first drag show. Oh, how he now had a better appreciation for Mama ChaCha and all she was. He had one night stands and he discovered glory holes—on campus and at the mall. He even had longer term "relationships" and "boyfriends," but no one he could ever bring home. It was still a secret and hidden world. A park-and-ride on a larger scale. These new friends, this new world, they did not really know him. They did not know his family and folks and the greater community of "home" because...well...*they would never allow it.*

Yet his visits home from college, or perhaps the new-found freedom of life away, allowed him to slip right into the comfortable anonymity of the park-and-ride and his old friends there, still meeting at the picnic tables...still swapping stories that our young man now recognized more as hunting or fishing tales, where the size of the rack or fish that may or may not have gotten away is discussed as an integral part of the story, and somehow growing and getting larger with each retelling. And he would share his tales and exploits and even pictures of boyfriends or "fuck buddies" he had met while away. He even brought one "roommate" back with him. And while it wasn't exactly a disaster, the tension at home was palpable, so that particular *never again* was a vow he never broke.

The friends at college and in D.C. (where he got his first "real job") seemed to rotate through the years. There were his drinking buddies from school, but they all sort of went their own way after graduation. And his grad school was sort of part-time, after work; he only met a few folks in a few classes there. Boyfriends, as they often do during one's twenties, came and went. (Pun both intended and not.) And even all the folks he started to socialize with at the office had other agendas and other lives and other plans—and often families of their own. He did not. And he was lonely.

The loss of his father brought him home. He left his "real job" to come and help his mother and his sister, and to help figure out the finances of the family farms. He left his buddies from the bars, his one friend in his apartment complex, and the guy he was sort of fucking, but it really wasn't going anywhere because the guy was sort of fucking another guy he was also sort of fucking—and who needs that kind of stupid sloppy-seconds bullcrap anyway?

It was about a month after he returned home and had settled a few financial items before he thought about the park-and-ride again. He looked into the lot one afternoon as he sped by on the highway. *My God, Mama ChaCha is still there.* He made a U-turn and found his way back to the circular lot. He pulled up to the familiar faded green Olds and got out to say hello to his old and dear friend.

"Well, hey stranger!" Mama ChaCha smiled. "Where've you been?"

"I was away for a bit...school, work, life," our hero answered; he was not so young now—at least he didn't feel young. And he would certainly balk at being called the hero of this story. "And now I'm back for awhile. It's been a month." His eyes seemed rather distant.

"What is it, son? Is somethin' wrong?"

Our hero looked at the kind and genuinely concerned man in front of him. He didn't understand what was happening to him— why he was suddenly feeling so lost and afraid—and his eyes grew wider as they struggled to hold the floodgates behind them. "My, uh, my dad died."

"Now honey, you listen to Mama, and you listen good.

You go on and take yourself a little walk back there. Bless your heart—you deserve it. And then come on back and tell Mama all about it once you get that part out of the way. You'll feel better."

And he did. He did take that walk, back towards the trees and trails, back towards the sweet quiet comfort of being lost in anonymity. No concerns, no responsibilities, and no expectations weighed on his shoulders.

And he did. He did come back and tell Mama all about it. He told Mama about the encounter he just had—a two-fer. He had eagerly joined in on the sport of two others. He talked about the guy he was seeing, or fucking, and how it was really going nowhere. He talked about his old job, and the ones he had now. Doing the books for his mom and helping his brother-in-law with the actual labor and day to day responsibilities of a large but slowly failing family farm. He talked about his dad....

And he did. He did feel better. He felt better after once again tasting a man he'd never met before. He felt better after his own pent-up frustration and anger and sadness and tension and fear and anxiety and sheer unadulterated horniness shot from his body, swallowed by a man he was pretty certain went to his father's funeral. And he felt better after the long and hearty cry he had while Mama ChaCha held him and told him it would all be okay.

<hr />

He swung by more regularly now. And he became one of the picnic table regulars. He chatted with Farmer Jeff on occasion. Farmer Jeff would talk his ear off, and did not always know when to stop talking so he could follow that hot piece that just wandered on back to the stream. He liked Black Jeff better. He didn't talk as much, and if you went by stereotypes, he probably had a bigger dick. Not that it mattered, because he never fooled around with either of the Jeffs. (But then again, dick size does matter—don't ever let some well-meaning girlfriend or wife tell you differently, because it does.)

One-Leg Mike didn't come around too often. But when he did, he always had some sordid tale to tell. He traveled a lot and was a kinky little thing. Sometimes our "young" man was a little grossed out by what One-Leg Mike would share, but he was always left with a great laugh, a huge smile, and just a tiny bit more curiosity as to any untold stories. Like rubbernecking at a bad accident, he swore he didn't want to see the worst, but, at the same time—he kinda did.

And last, but certainly not least, was One-Eyed Sally. Holy fuck, yeah, that was a cock. He touched it once, while some old guy was going back and forth, servicing the two of them, but he never went beyond that. It was just too damn big. (And I know I just said size matters, but this was extreme.) Perhaps you've heard people describe a rather large penis as being like a baby's arm? Well, this was more like the forearm of a grown-ass adult, a grown-ass WWE wrestler adult.

It was AIDS that ultimately took One-Eyed Sally. AIDS, or the many complications thereof, took a lot of lives as it spread through the anonymity of hidden and clandestine encounters. Even if it didn't take them, per se, it changed them. One is never the same watching the vibrant life of a young virile friend slowly drained, like the slow leak of an unattended coolant reservoir; one must always take care.

Yet the shadow of AIDS, in and of itself, was not capable of bringing a close to this secretive park-and-ride life. No, the denizens of these woods and those of other places, and even times, have always found ways to survive amongst the shadows of the everyday in the USA. Practices and precautions and sometimes the open and complete honesty that can only come from these unchaste, unfaithful, unreserved fornications offered a protective shroud.

Clearings along the paths and the creekbed often held the evidence of such couplings, if indeed the affair was limited to two. Often it was not. Torn foil squares and a vast array of latex sheaths, all colors of the rainbow and a few other textured shades that perhaps one would prefer to have gone unseen were an oddly comforting sight amongst the empty bottles of beer and booze. Sometimes a magazine would be found, most times just a torn page. Random evidence of drug use and forgotten items of clothing offered a more disturbing tale.

But it was when the guy who drove the blue Subaru was murdered that things started to really change. Oh, the speculation and the scandal—he was a local guy with a family, and after the discovery of his body, he was no longer anonymous. The official word from the family was that he had an "addiction to prescription drugs" and that "this was the sad result of a desperate and naive man finding himself in a drug deal gone wrong."

The speculation and scandal came about as the park-and-ride was familiar not to just those who parked and rode, but to everyone else in town as well. "You can always swing by the park-and-ride for a blowie," you may recall. The police, the community at large, the family of the poor deceased man, and of course the "regulars" all wanted answers.

It was Mama ChaCha who had the real answer. As Mama, our hero, and a friend of Mama's he hadn't met before sat talking near the picnic tables one day, there was still a lot of activity about the creek and the trees. And not the activity that we might all be thinking; no—there was still the bright yellow crime scene tape. And there were still cops. Gone were the news crews and cameras which had kept many folks away from the park-and-ride for weeks. It was difficult to maintain the anonymity of the park-and-ride when one was on the local news. But now there were landscape crews and tree trimmers instead of reporters. There was a lot of activity, indeed.

"I know what happened," Mama ChaCha offered.

The other man at the table, the one our hero did not know, laughed. "How do you know what happened, Mama?"

"One-Eyed Sally told me." Mama nodded seriously. "Girl, she was here that night."

"When?" our hero asked.

"The night that man went and got himself murdered."

"No...!" Our hero was enthralled by this wild bit of gossip, "When did One-Eyed Sally tell you this?"

Mama ChaCha blushed. The man burst out laughing and Mama uttered a few harsh criticisms toward him while the younger man looked back and forth between the two. He cracked a curious smile.

"Holy crap, you and One-Eyed Sally?" he asked.

"Girl, it's not the first time," Mama fanned himself with his hand.

"How?" the younger one asked, wide-eyed.

It was the man he didn't know who answered this one. "Poppers."

"Now, you behave." Mama scolded before turning serious. "Now, what I heard was that he came here like he always did. Girlfriend wasn't addicted to prescription drugs, Lord no, she was addicted to dick. That's what she was addicted to."

"So it wasn't a drug deal gone bad?" the younger man asked.

"Nope, just a blow and go gone no" laughed the other man.

"Oh no. Bless his heart—it was kinda both." Mama ChaCha shook his head. "Poor dumb fool thought he was walking back to the woods to suck that man's dick. But that man just thought he was gonna buy some drugs."

"I guess neither of them got what they wanted," our younger man quipped.

"I heard it was more than his mouth that got fucked before the dude was knifed," the man said in a lower, not quite hushed voice, "And that it wasn't pretty."

And that was all but the end of that particular park-and-ride. Almost.

―――◇―――

In fact, the park-and-ride went through a major overhaul after that unfortunate exchange by the creek in the woods. First, it was the increased police presence. Farmer Jeff actually called Black Jeff one night for bail money (He couldn't exactly call his wife.) Yeah, that picnic table crew really had to step up their game of looking out for one another. From a heads up while giving head to back-up in case you meet one of those self-loathing closet cases who are hell bent on beating up a fag—after, of course, they had their dick sucked. Or better yet, after they sucked said fag's dick.

The scandal of the murder brought a lot of curioity seekers and first-timers to the park-and-ride. Some came to gawk and laugh at the queers as though they were some new zoo exhibit in their natural habitat. A few even ventured further, making it a rather friendly petting zoo—if one were to push the metaphor, so to speak. Some came to condemn or judge. Oh, the bible thumpers that tried to hold vigils at the park-and-ride—only the tables would turn and they would appear to be the imprisoned animals as the picnic table crew would laugh and taunt.

But it was the work crews that did the most to alter the park-and-ride experience. First it was the resurfacing and lighting. Mama wondered if they might start holding nighttime sporting events, not that he would mind. He appreciated sports. He was even in a football pool with a group of friends, some of whom were from the park-and-ride. It is true—gay folks love sports. And not just those lesbians who are always coaches and physical education teachers at public schools across the nation, or the long list of other stereotypes: figure skaters, dancers, gymnasts,....

Of course Mama ChaCha chose his favorites by the roundest tight end and the hottest quarterback. "Ooh honey, I don't need you to be my quarterback; I need you to do me bareback!" Mama ChaCha did not feel the need to challenge stereotypes.

After the lights and resurfacing came the chainsaws.

The trees were taken down, nearly all of them. A few of the larger ones were left; at least they offered some shade if no longer camouflage. And that oft whispered phrase—"You can always swing by the park-and-ride for a blowie"—now, more often than not, it led to disappointment.

One of the final nails was the sale of the farmland next door. It was sold to a developer, and a large business park was brought in. It added more light, fewer trees, and even less opportunity. The park-and-ride was no longer a blow and go. It was a meet and greet—and then take that shit elsewhere before you got caught. But it was something else, too.

———◇———

Pulling into the park-and-ride, our hero—no longer the boy he was, and really no longer a "young" man—couldn't help but smile. There, parked beneath a lucky tree spared by the chainsaw, was that faded and worn green Olds, bathed in the colors of fall as the leaves seemed to blanket Mama's car. *How long has he been here?* Stepping up to the car he found Mama in repose, mouth open, newspaper sprawled across his chest.

"I'm not dead, God dammit!"

The younger man laughed. "You're still coming here, Mama? After all these years?"

"Of course, child. Now you know I like to read my paper and take a nap."

"Well that's about all you can do since the trees are gone," the young man laughed. It felt good to laugh. "What do you and your legendary tongue do now?"

"Now that's just nasty; you stop!" Mama scolded. "You know that's not why I come here."

"I believe One-Eyed Sally and some poppers tell a different story."

"I am your mother!"

Our younger man was laughing harder now, and so was Mama ChaCha. "So why do you come here, Mama?"

"I come here to see my friends," Mama ChaCha said simply.

They shared the silence for a while, before talking about this and that. Mama ChaCha educated our friend on all the doings of the picnic table crew and all the happenings in the community: stories of Farmer Jeff and Black Jeff, and the misadventures of One-Leg Mike. Mama shared his own stories of work, car repairs, and time spent with friends. He did mention a few encounters of the more amorous kind, including an ongoing tet-a-tet of sorts with a local waterman and of the passing of One-Eyed Sally.

"I'm sorry about your mother." Mama ChaCha suddenly said, and took the younger man's hand.

Our hero's eyes were red and flooded with tears before he could even register what it was Mama ChaCha had said. And then he collapsed into his Mama's arms, just the way he had when he told Mama about the heartache of his first crush. Just the way he had after that man he Ubered home with from the bar that night, an older guy—he gave up to that man something he had given to no other. Mama ChaCha ended up meeting our friend at his truck the next morning. He had lost his keys and the man who fucked him didn't have time to help; the man he Ubered with just dropped him off at his truck. Oh, and as it turns out, the man was married. He cried into Mama ChaCha's arms like he did when he lost his dad. And now it was his mother he had lost. And he cried. And Mama held him, and rocked him, and told him it would all be okay.

"I read it in the obituaries," Mama whispered.

Our younger man couldn't help but snort a snot-filled laugh into Mama's chest.

Mama slapped him lovingly on the back of his head. "Now girl, you know I love my obituaries."

"I know you do." The younger man laughed, kissing Mama ChaCha on the cheek.

"And you know I love my family," Mama ChaCha said simply once more.

"I love you, Mama ChaCha." He hugged Mama and kissed his cheek again.

"Now that's enough of that!" Mama ChaCha beamed. "Tell me all about the dick you're getting...."

And he did. And the two friends chatted well into the night. Black Jeff showed up with a tray of milkshakes, while Farmer Jeff brought take out. One-Leg Mike had a pizza delivered straight to the picnic tables. And folks came and went. And no one went to the creek, and no one had a blow and go. To be fair, a few folks did go in order to have the blow somewhere else. But mostly they just sat and shared and laughed and loved. It was a good, old-fashioned, queer little block party for friends and family—at the local park-and-ride.

Lesson 2:

It gets better when we step out
of the closet, find our light,
and let it shine.

"For those troubled LGBTQ people who need someone to talk to, someone to accept them — let them know they are loved. Help the young ones, and even the older ones coming out, and give that support.

Stormy Vain

"I spent too many years in the closet. I deserve a fabulous wardrobe."

Missy

The Textbook Closet

You could hear it in the halls:

"Faggot!"

"Hey, Fag!"

"Gay boy."

"Sissy"

"Queer bait!"

That last one was the one I never really understood. "Queer bait." Like what are you—bait for queers? I guess that's what they were getting at, but it all just seemed all so stupid to me. Then again, boys are stupid. And mean. At least in high school. And we were in high school.

I was a "smart and pretty" black girl from a small southern town in north central Florida. At least that's what I was told. Sometimes I was pretty without the smart, and sometimes I was just smart without the pretty—but I was always black. That was life in a small southern town. We were about twenty miles away from the University of Florida, where the Gators played championship football in The Swamp. On one of those scorchers of a day, where the temperature hovered around the century mark, and the humidity was barely a percentage point below; where, with every breath you took, it felt like your face was wrapped in cheesecloth that had been dipped in warm mayonnaise—it was easy to see why it's known as The Swamp.

We were mostly an agricultural community. Tobacco was a big crop, and there was all sorts of other produce. Florida has always had the gift of multiple growing seasons, and our community, communities really, provided ample labor. I say communities because, really, there were four. A deep and segregated divide existed—race and economics being the barriers. There was the middle-to-upper class white community and then there were their poorer, less educated, often disowned, discarded, or ignored relations. And there was the middle class black community of which I was a part. While we had similar relations as the white folks with regard to education and economics, we tended to still acknowledge our own as kin. It always cracked me up when a certain white lady with a certain last name would deny any connection to those *other* certain white folks with that same certain last name. And then, God forbid, should you even mention the black families who also shared that certain last name. People like to think Florida is all sunshine and beaches when, really, sunshine and beaches are just the edge pieces of the puzzle. There is a whole lot going on in the middle.

Desegregation was not a smooth transition in these small, rural southern towns to say the least, despite the fact that it was a veritable family reunion for many communities who now found themselves shopping with, dining with, and going to school with all sorts of folks with that same certain last name. One solution for white people was to employ the use of private schools, so many private schools opened across the United States in the late '60s and early '70s as communities were coming to the realization that this was not going away. Those private schools were roughly 99.9% white, of course. I went to public school.

By the time I reached middle school which, ironically, was housed in the old black high school back in the day, we were saying goodbye to the '80s. You could say that the '80s had had their magical pastel and glitter effect on just about everything. An economic downturn all but killed the private school in our town, and my seventh grade year found me amongst a whole host of new folks and friends. And I do mean friends. The '80s made it sort of uncool to be openly racist. And the best way not to be an open racist, of course, was to have a black friend. As I mentioned earlier, I was a "smart and pretty" black girl. I had so many white friends with all sorts of last names. I had my black friends too, of course. And my family. And I was reminded daily by all of them where I came from and who I was.

And so too, it seems, was the new kid—for apparently he was the "bait" about which I spoke earlier. He was the one about whom those whispers, those comments, those shouts, those threats were made. And he really wasn't "the new kid," not anymore. I mean he moved to town during middle school, and we were now in high school. But that moniker, like the others, seemed to stick.

Do y'all remember that being a big deal? When a new kid came? Well, in a small southern town with about a dozen and a half last names, it's a big deal! And what was even more amazing—he didn't start the year, or even come in after Christmas break; he just showed up in late April, with about a month and a half of school left. Maybe that's why he stood out. Well, that, and he was different.

We didn't have the same homeroom, and we didn't share a lot of classes when he started at the middle school. I remember an altercation he had with my cousin in math class, though. He sat at the back table across from my cousin; he was new and the teacher didn't assign him a desk, only a chair at the table normally used for group work or problem students. My cousin was dancing around him, asking him all sorts of rude questions, and she was doing that thing where you hold your hands real close to a person and tell them repeatedly that you aren't touching them. He sat stone faced, this skinny little white boy who I believed at the time had been plucked from one of those private schools and dropped here unceremoniously and...he simply did not understand why. My cousin was getting her evil little thrill until he did something no other skinny little white boy or girl did—he hit her. Now, normally, I would go ape shit over a man hitting a woman, especially if that woman was family, but they were both twelve. Also, without exaggeration, she was more than twice his size. And she was a known fighter. She had just returned from being suspended for jumping a girl in the bathroom. And she had it coming—my cousin, not the girl in the bathroom. That suspension was over a barrette.

It all happened so fast. One second, she was dancing and telling him she wasn't touching him while the teacher was at his desk reading a book; and the rest of us were working on our worksheets, receiving the finest Florida public education money could buy. The next second, this skinny little white boy was on his feet. His chair had flipped over with the sudden force of his movement. It was evident he had just punched my cousin in the boob. Every head turned in unison, and the teacher's face took an even chalkier hue, as he was certain he would lose his job after this enormous black girl pummeled this tiny white kid into a greasy spot on the floor. Our collective breath was held as the two stared at each other. The white boy said something to my cousin that no one heard.

"Ooops, my bad, I slipped. You alright?" She said to the kid.

"No no. It's all good," he said.

And then they sat back down at the table and started on their worksheets. The teacher made a lame attempt at a joke or admonishment we couldn't quite hear, but mostly he sat back down and returned to his book. The bell rang. Both my cousin and the new boy were surrounded by the folks you would expect as they walked to their respective classes. They all wanted to know what happened.

"Nothing" was the answer from both.

They had a strange relationship after that. My cousin developed a deep and borderline obsessive infatuation with him, claiming to me on many occasions that she would marry him one day. He was just always kind to her. They would talk in the hall sometimes, and even ate lunch together. And they kept this up all the way through high school. They had a special bond, but he never led her on. He was always clear they were friends. And they were...they were friends.

He had to be just 16 or 17 now, that new kid from middle school—I'm trying to remember what year it was, our junior or senior year of high school? I'm pretty sure it was our senior year. He was, I don't want to say he was special, that's not quite it. And it comes with a whole host of connotations...but he was. He was different than any other boy I knew at that high school. In that town. Really, in my life. He was president of the drama club, which is funny because he always seemed to do everything he could to disappear while in class or walking down the halls. But wow, when he was on stage, he was someone different. He was a loud crazy person or a sympathetic little brother or a charming and witty leading man. At least in the manner in which a high school theatre production of anything can have a charming and witty leading man. He could cry on stage when the role called for tears. He won some big award for acting, I vaguely remember; It was from the state and not from the school. He was good, there was no doubt. But I think the biggest part he played was the one he played every single day at school.

He had friends, don't get me wrong. I mean, outside of my cousin. I'd even like to think we were friends. Or friendly anyway. But he had his drama friends, his friends from classes. He was smart and we shared a lot of the honors classes. But as I mentioned before, he was the recipient of a lot of whispers and name-calling and out and out confrontation a few times. Once, one of the bigger and taller and redneckier boys decided he would stand in the doorway and not let the new kid into the room. It was Algebra class. You could hear the slight commotion, the taunting, the name calling, the "So whaddya gonna do about it, faggot?"

Those of us who could hear the altercation sat in various stages of embarrassment or awkwardness and tried to pretend it wasn't happening. And the teacher, well—she ignored it too. She just kept writing a series of math problems on the board. The bell rang, and the new kid was still trapped outside in the open air hallway of a typical Florida school. Our teacher looked annoyed, but she kept writing and only turned her head after we all heard, "So fucking hit me or beat me up or whatever. I don't care, just fucking move." And he pushed the bully backward into the class. The giant didn't fall—it was just a few missteps. A skinny boy caught a mountain of a much larger boy off guard with his words and a quick shove. At that point our teacher turned around, red-faced, and scolded them both for playing out in the hall.

It was around that time when a fellow cheerleading

friend of mine and I were asked to help the new kid with a thing—a song and dance routine for talent night. For us, it was a chance to miss class and some other useless senior year assignment. For him, it was a chance to try something out of his "comfort zone"—to "push himself." At least that's what he said. A lot. He said it at every one of our rehearsals. It wasn't practice; he always insisted we call it rehearsal. He was determined, hard working, and very businesslike about it.

And he wasn't terrible. But he also wasn't good. Not at all. We did our best to make a routine that was less dance and more spin, twirl, jump, and tap your foot. He could do those things; at least he had a tiny bit of rhythm. And if the music was turned up really loud, well, you couldn't hear him sing. So that also worked to his benefit.

We did this for about two weeks, these rehearsals—and then it was the night of the talent show. The other girls and I were doing a new cheer routine we had learned at a cheer camp with the U of F cheerleading squad post-football season. We were backstage with the other talent show participants. And I saw him.

He was talking to the drama teacher and it did not look like a pleasant discussion. The teacher looked unusually frustrated, being the nicest woman in the world, and he looked defiant and adamant. Her eyes caught mine and I knew she wanted me to walk over and offer some help. I did. I walked over and our teacher stepped back and let me try to talk to him. I looked at him and asked what was wrong. He said he couldn't do this.

I was like, "What? Go out there? You do it all the time. How can *you* be nervous?"

"I can't do this. This is not me." He kept saying that over

and over, quietly, to himself.

I recalled how hard he'd worked, how hard we'd all worked. And I reminded him about what he had said about his comfort zone and trying something different and pushing himself. But he kept repeating those words. "This is not me."

And then came the clapping, some cheers, and some applause. He looked at me, he looked at our teacher; the act on the stage had ended. We both stood in the wings looking at that empty dark stage. Our teacher walked back over to us, and told him to go; that was his cue. He turned and looked at me again, our eyes met, and …

BAM, I was suddenly in middle school again. I was just a young local middle school girl and he was the quiet and sometimes shy, skinny new boy; and we were alone in the textbook closet.

I had library with him back then. Outside of that math class, it was the only class I had with him in middle school. It was an elective we could take. We learned the Dewey Decimal System and we learned all the parts of a book. And it was a study hall, really, and we shelved books so the librarian didn't have to; at least that's how we kids looked at it. So it really was a blow-off class—that is, until we had to do an inventory of all the books. A very boring job of counting and categorizing all the books in the library, the classrooms, and on this particular day we were asked to go to the textbook closet. The textbook closet was really a small classroom or office lined with shelves and boxes holding all the textbooks in the entire history of the school. And me and the new kid had to count them.

It was early June; school would be over in a week, and it

was one of those hot and swampy, "mayonnaise-and-cheese-cloth" kind of days. Our library skills class was in the after-noon, the hottest time of the day, and we had the wall air conditioning unit cranked on its coldest setting. I picked up a box of books to slide it over a bookshelf to him. I was on one side of the shelf, and he was on the other. As the box slid across the top of the shelf, he took it, and the bottom gave out. He fell backwards, buried under a small avalanche of sixth grade science books.

He laughed and I laughed as he stood and our eyes met. There was a brief pause as our laughter turned to smiles and then turned to just staring—and so I leaned forward across the shelf, lips puckered, and I went in for the kiss. He stood wide-eyed and frozen, unsure of how to proceed. It was a moment of timidness or awkwardness or perhaps even stage fright, but he stood there—paralyzed. It was like the world had frozen still for him, for just a moment. And as I was about to kiss him, I saw the desire in his eyes—the yearning to do this one small thing, to just lean forward and kiss this smart pretty girl.

"I can't do this. This is not me." I could also see *that* in his eyes.

I leaned in further, our lips met, and we kissed. Well, I kissed him. We both took a step back, a deep breath, and then we proceeded with what we were doing. The kissing. Then the bell rang, and the librarian walked in to give us grief for not being back in the library before class ended. We played it off like we were picking up books from the floor. We got hall passes to our next classes because we were going to be late—and that was that.

Things were awkward after that. Like that moment

39

before our first kiss. I feel like if I had just stepped forward again, if I had just leaned once more at some other textbook closet opportune time, well maybe something else would have happened. But I didn't, and nothing else happened. The summer came. And that moment was all but forgotten.

"I can't. I can't do this. This is not me." I heard those words again. He may even have said them to himself. They may not have been out loud, but I could hear them loud and clear as I looked in his pleading eyes.

At that moment years ago, in that middle school textbook closet, I leaned in and kissed him. In this moment, in the wings of the high school backstage, I just wanted to reach out and hug him. Hold him. Tell him not to be anything he didn't want to be. Not to try to be someone he wasn't no matter how happy it made others. I saw the fear and the confusion and the anger and I just wanted to make it all okay. But I didn't. I couldn't. I just stood there and watched as our teacher placed her hand on the small of his back and gave him a little push.

The lights came on and they were really bright. He couldn't see the audience. And the music was loud and they couldn't really hear him sing. He twirled, and jumped, and spun in all the right places. It was a terrible mix of tumbling, modern dance, and cheer. And thankfully there were not too many people there. So he wasn't made fun of too much in the weeks that followed. I never joined in and I'm embarrassed to say I never really defended him, either. I just rolled my eyes and walked away.

I knew something different, though, about that boy. He could live through the humiliation of the dance. He had walls he had built around himself, a super thick skin he had developed for those sorts of moments. He had ignored name-calling and taunts before this and he would go on to ignore them after. That part was not new. What he wasn't prepared for was my seeing him. And for a second time, he let slip who he truly was at a very specific and vulnerable moment—and I wasn't prepared to recognize that I was seeing him. For two brief moments I saw this boy terrified, because he was caught being who he was.

It was at that moment in high school when I knew what being gay must be like. Or as much as a "smart and pretty" and straight black girl from the South can, anyway. Being gay was not the jokes or the stereotypes or the clothes or the sex that seemed so unnatural to so many. It was not the bullying or the abuse or the name-calling. It was waking up everyday, looking in the mirror, seeing yourself and knowing...*I can't do this. This is not me.* And it was the realization that you grow up, denying and hiding a part of you, and pretending to be what others want. It is choosing this mask or that one; adapting to one thing or another. Evolving and twisting and changing so you can fit in, and you are so practiced and so convincing that even you forget which parts are real and which parts are an act—and which parts are put away, deep within that closet.

There is safety in the closet. I can see that now. I felt safe enough to lean across the shelf and kiss that white boy. If it weren't for that textbook closet, I may never have felt so brave. I'm sure this is just an overthought or overwrought analogy, but there is something about the knowledge I gained in that closet that didn't come from the volumes of books within its walls.

There is safety in the closet, sure—that's why we put things there. To keep them safe, and hidden away. There is a lot of discovery, too, tucked away in the volumes and boxes and shelves and unruly piles of textbooks. But there is no truth tucked away in the unread pages of a sixth grade science book, no freedom in an eighth grade history book, and no comfort in the stories we are asked to read about people who look nothing like us...who *are* nothing like us. Eventually what is inside must come out. It might be when the bottom of the box gives way or when that guiding hand shoves us into the unwelcome spotlight. It might even be when we exchange a glance, or a look, or a simple sweet and innocent first kiss.

Lesson 3:

---◇---

Life is short. Things come and go
so you might as well
unbutton your fly..

---◇---

"Always get a dick pic up front."

Ms. P

"Casual sex? I don't know, I'm married!"

Fheanix Fischer

Unbutton Your Fly

"Button your fly?" he asked as I walked past his car. A small sporty looking thing, but nothing really fancy. It wasn't a convertible. It wasn't red. And it wasn't one of those mid-life crisis cars that screamed, "Look, my bank account and credit score can still get it up!" No, it was a bit more subdued, a bit more beat up. And it had a little mileage on it, kind of like the owner. It was more along the lines of "I just came into some money, but it turns out it wasn't quite as much as I initially thought, and I'm not sure if I will be getting any more, so *this* is the car I got."

I paused and squinted through the glare off the windshield of his little ride. A few clouds aloft in the watery blue sky, some tree branches and palm fronds dancing in the breeze. The expressway served as the backdrop to my silhouette like a reflection painted in the glass.

"Unbutton your fly."

"Excuse me?" I asked, stepping forward and now looking into the open passenger window. His tall, lean frame filled the driver side seat, which was pushed almost into the back seat of his little coupe. I was now reflected in the lenses of his wire framed "cop glasses." I knew there was an actual name for these sunglasses—aviators, maybe? But they were the kind that the guys always wore on that show *C.H.I.P.S.*, so I always just called them cop glasses.

"Button your fly?" Again he inquired; a slight wink, a moustachioed smile, and an inviting nod toward the seat beside him. "Unbutton your fly."

45

The look of confusion must have been all over my face. He assumed I misunderstood him or that I didn't know what he was talking about. He was correct. I didn't. But that's not what I was focussed on or why my face wore the confused and strained look. I'd seen this man before and I could not remember where.

"Your shirt," he said.

I looked down. Clarity. Sweet clarity. I was wearing a faded black t-shirt with blue lettering that read "Button Your Fly."

I looked back up at him, "Oh, right." I sort of laughed, still struggling to place his face. *Where had I seen him before?*

"Well?" He was smiling a broad smile now.

He had a rather thin face, dark curly hair, and one of those complexions that always look like they have a slight tan even when they clearly don't. Olive-skinned they call it though I don't know why; he was neither black nor green. His teeth were white but sort of horse-like, and they were hidden by a super thick pornstache. You know the kind, where you feel like he should be delivering a pizza or maybe he's just here to check your plumbing.

"I feel like I know you. Have we met?" I asked with a hesitant sort of smile.

"Why don't you have a seat?" He offered through the open window, leaning back further into the cracked pleather. He opened his own denim-clad thighs wider and gave them a cool little slap as he sat back.

My hand found the warm silver door handle and gave it a pull. "I can't."

"Why not?" His brow furrowed, disappointment revealed over his Ponch glasses.

I snapped the handle again, making it a bit more clear. It was locked.

His long, lean frame reached over and grasped the small silver knob that had proven to be my impediment. His Nosferatu meets Andre the Giant fingers, unable to grasp the smooth and short metal head of the lock, slipped and slid as he fumbled.

"It's sorta broke on this side." An embarrassed, breathy, muffled sort of laugh escaped his lips; his teeth peeking through his moustache like a nosy neighbor on the other side of drawn drapes. He was suddenly as red-faced and embarrassed as I felt I was, leaning awkwardly toward the low window, suddenly aware of just how crowded and popular this park seemed to be.

If it were a sportier car or if he were a hunkier guy, *Magnum P.I.* fantasies would have abounded. However, he was more like that cartoon character Horace Horsecollar than he was a hirsute private eye in short shorts and an open shirt tearing across Hawaii. He finally managed to unlock the door with one hand while his other rested demonstrably beside a rather large and long and unnatural looking bulge. It literally snaked down the thigh of his jeans. Horse Hung Horace may not have a Ferrari, but it looked as if he sure as hell could stretch out a Magnum. I got in.

I closed the door and turned to him. Instantly his large hands and fingers went to the button at the top of my jeans. Ironically, they were not 501s and they did not have a button fly, but he didn't seem to catch or care about the irony.

"Button your fly; unbutton your fly," he played with the words once more. He was *really* into his joke. And he was also *really* into getting inside my pants. I think this was his suave and clever way of asking for my assistance as he was having no more luck with my top button than he'd had with the lock on his door.

Nervous as I was, I managed to lean back farther into the seat. His free hand fumbled at the side of the seat and I found myself falling back. I suddenly collapsed into a reclining position. There was a hard and uncomfortable prodding, pushing hard against my backside. I was rather confused as this olive-skinned bean pole was more or less on top of me, still struggling to get his fingers and my button to come to an understanding. I shifted a bit, and I pulled the seat belt buckle from its attempted violation. We shifted some more. Suddenly, I had an entirely different view. And oh boy, was I mesmerized by the now even longer snake along his thigh. I was also enjoying the attention he was giving my own growing friend, trapped as it was by the waistband of the jeans he had yet to figure out how to unfasten, my hip, and his incredibly large and persistent hand. I had by now given up on the notion that I'd seen him before. Or perhaps I simply stopped caring as I pushed him off me, adjusted positions, and then attempted to take my own turn on the impossible beast now before me.

If the scenario weren't so seedy—the sporty-ish little car belonging to Horace Horsecollar, Horace and his Magnum, me and my eagerness parked so out in the open here—a popular park near an up-and-coming neighborhood; joggers and walkers doing their health thing with a few stopping at the strategically placed activity benches where one could do sit ups or squats or pull ups or some other exercise the forward-thinking urban planner had designed. There was some guy standing on the shore of the lake fishing for goodness knows what three-eyed scaly thing he might pull from this urban lake wedged between that neighborhood and the expressway. There was the post-rush-hour early evening traffic roaring across the expressway that passed over the far edge of this rather large sinkhole called a lake. A family picnic; a cop walking our way. If it weren't so seedy, well, it would have been just hilarious!

With the grace and subtlety of a newborn giraffe trying to walk in heels, I quickly pulled myself away from what could have been the neck of said newborn giraffe and tried to be casual about it. Sitting flustered and red-faced, heart pounding, and my throat feeling as though an intubation tube had been yanked out by a nurse named Ratched, or maybe Annie. (No, *Ratched*, as I don't think Annie had been written yet.) Anyway, I tried to be casual. My friend with the Alaskan pipeline reached behind my seat and grabbed an old wadded up t-shirt, stiff and stained, and draped it across his lap. And that was enough for me.

As the officer passed us by, suspiciously yet carelessly glancing through the front windshield at us, I gambled he was met with the same glare and reflection I was and I bailed. I fixed my unbuttoned fly and climbed from the low sporty Ferrari wannabe, stood, and casually adjusted myself into something more acceptable to the staring eyes of the picnic family. I turned back and leaned through the still open window; I wondered if it was broken, too. I began apologizing, saying how weirded out I was by the cop and that I just couldn't get caught; he leaned forward across the passenger seat and tried to kiss me through the window. I stood up, hit my head on the roof of his ride, and I stepped back. He smiled and gave me a little wink, but his small brown eyes looked sad. He retrieved his cop glasses from the dash, started his car—it took a few tries—and slowly pulled away.

◄———◆———►

It was sometime later—years, a decade, maybe more, probably more. Time is a tricky and unreliable thing in one's memory, and even more so when trying to remember one's early twenties. It was much later when I came across my well-hung friend again. I was chatting with another friend, an actual friend. It was a stupid text exchange about an even stupider guy he was hoping to date.

I made a "Size Queen" joke reminding him of his penchant for all things super-sized. He sent a gif of some lady rolling her eyes. I sent an eggplant emoji that was laughing while crying. My friend then sent another gif—it was Horace! Only his name wasn't Horace in the gif. And he was buried what, for some, would have been elbow deep inside some blonde twink clinging to a piece of exercise equipment.

And it all came crashing back to me—that very first time I saw him. It was in a magazine I had picked up at an adult bookstore down a little dirt road off the highway, near the college. I was all red-faced and flustered and shaking when I walked into that store. I nervously looked around at racks of magazines and books, blow-up dolls and dildos, images of large breasts and open vaginas everywhere until the middle-aged lady behind the counter sort of smiled a knowing smile. "We sell these too, hon. I think it might be what you are looking for." And she pointed at a spinning metal rack that held various magazines. I chose a three-pack, wrapped in clear plastic, covered in X's and attractive muscular men. That guy from the park graced the cover of one of those magazines—an homage to big-dicked porn stars.

After I graduated from red-faced magazine purchases, I remembered a few VHS tapes I rented back in the day. Still red-faced and shaky, I would walk into those little rooms walled off from the rest of the video rental store. I'd look on *that* shelf that was completely out of the way and still feel as though everyone was watching me—and they were. Well, Horace was a member of the talented ensemble in a few of those star-studded films as well.

And here I was, scrolling through my phone, researching and reading about "vintage" pornstars, as one does when they realize they may or may not have had a seedy little encounter with one. He was a gay porn star known for playing "Dominant Daddy" types—and known for the size of his tool. He was also known to be a prissy little bottom when not on camera and a diva and a pain in the ass (no pun intended) on the set. And he was known by some to be kind, gentle, funny, and caring— and he was also known to be dead. Sometime in the early 2000s. It was AIDS.

For many, coming of age in the '80s and '90s was like a game of Spin the Bottle. You know, where kids sit in a circle and the bottle is spun and the spinner has to lean forward and kiss whomever the bottle neck pointed to. And for others, for so many gay men, it was like adding an element of Russian Roulette to the table. I have spun that bottle countless times. And I have held that gun to my head more times than I care to remember. But I never took a bullet. I was one of the lucky ones. I got chlamydia once, from a girl; isn't that ironic? I'll bet Alanis never put that in a song.

I still own a pair of 501s. They don't really fit quite like they used to, or the way I remember them fitting. But then again, when I look in the mirror I don't always remember my body looking this way either. And I do not have the t-shirt, not anymore. It has long ago gone to that great t-shirt hamper in the sky. "Button your fly" it read.

"Unbutton your fly. ..."

Lesson 4:

―――――◇―――――

A mother always knows
that shoes make the man ...

―――――◇―――――

"Go two sizes up and pray!"

Vickie Fischer

"Bless your heart,
you always gotta make it so hard."

Mama ChaCha

Shoes Make the Man

Margaret Anne was a no-nonsense, straightforward woman of selective speech. Selective speech? Yes; I'll clarify: By selective speech, I mean that she was a woman of few words but many, many thoughts. When she spoke, it was always wise to listen. Her emotions, much like her words, were rarely shared. She preferred to keep these personal things to herself.

Well, on this particular morning, she woke up excited. Absolutely excited and thrilled to be having lunch with her son today. It was nothing special, just takeout from a local sandwich shop chain attached to the local gas station chain. But it was a convenient stop on the way to his new home. And they made the best cheesesteak with grilled onions on this side of the whole county.

Jimmy, her most successful child, had recently purchased a fairly new, single-wide trailer and rented a small lot. It's not that Margaret Anne's other children are not successful. Each of them have had their own series of successes and failures through the years, as have we all. And I assure you Jimmy has moved beyond his "single-wide trailer on a rented lot" days (not that there's anything wrong with that.) But on this particular day, at this particular time, Jimmy was only 21 years old. And he had paid for this trailer with his own money, while attending college, and working; he also managed not to get any girlfriends pregnant. And Margaret Ann was especially proud of that.

Margaret Anne got out of bed and did her normal slow

shuffle to the bathroom. She stared at her reflection and the same much older stranger stared back. Was it just the teeth that made her look so old? A history of bad teeth, bad gums, and bad choices left her pushing 50 with a full set of dentures already. But it wasn't that. She was used to that look. And besides, after popping in her teeth, the same older face still stared back. So it wasn't the teeth.

No. She realized as she washed her face that it was the smile. Her years of stress and worry over her children and her husband did not show on her face when she looked annoyed. At least not in the form of wrinkles and lines—not like when she smiled. And yet she could not help but smile. And it made her uneasy. So she went back to her safety net, her routine. She started breakfast for her husband, Ralph. He liked a full breakfast every morning. And so she made one.

"What's with you?" Ralph was sitting at the table with his coffee, watching as his wife made his breakfast.

"What do you mean?" Margaret Anne cracked an egg on the griddle beside the sizzling slice of scrapple.

"Don't break it." He barked around a mouthful of coffee.

"I never do."

"That face. What's that face?" Ralph suddenly took notice of his wife. "Don't get the egg too close to the scrapple; you'll break it."

"I don't know." Margaret Anne mumbled. She was implementing her "selective speaking" in its full capacity.

"You gotta fart?"

"It's a smile. I'm happy."

"Whaddya got to be so happy about?"

Margaret Anne flipped Ralph's egg and pressed it hard

to the bottom of the pan.

"That's it, kill it." Ralph coached.

"I'm going down to Jimmy's today at lunch. I'm picking up cheesesteaks on the way."

"What am I supposed to do for lunch?"

"Best thing I can tell you to do is be nice to one of your daughters if standing there telling me how to cook for you all these years hasn't taught you how to fry your own egg." Margaret Anne looked as though she might pass gas again.

"Now you know I can make them fried turkey tenderloin and...."

"Oh, good. So you won't go hungry." Less than gently, she placed his plate of eggs and scrapple on the table.

Ralph knew it was time to stop talking and eat his breakfast.

———◆———

Jimmy woke up excited. Ever since moving into his own place he woke up that way. He was thrilled by the freedom of it all, of course, but mostly he was filled with pride. He had made quite a few sacrifices living at home, banking his money while he worked, all while going to school. His friends and coworkers had their own places, and they gave Jimmy the business over still living at home.

"You are just a mama's boy; nothin' wrong in that," one of his friends would often say.

But mostly, those friends of his rented. And while he was the last of them all to still be living at home with mom and dad, he had paid cash for his first car when he was just 15 years old, before he could even legally drive. And he had just paid cash for this mobile home at the age of 21. It wasn't the greatest or most luxurious of accommodations, but it was fairly new, it was clean, and it was more than any of his friends actually owned.

And it was Halloween—or almost Halloween. And Halloween was one of his favorite holidays. He loved to dress up. He loved the attention that being in a costume brought, attention he shied away from when in his regular attire or persona. And he did have his friend's party to go to that night. Bobby always had the best parties. There would be a whole bunch of folks there; many he knew, and many he did not. A big ol' table of food, more booze than was necessary, and a few other items or moments of interest. It was the other items and moments that intrigued 21 year-old Jimmy. It was a costume party, of course, and Jimmy was really coming out tonight. He had worked hard on his costume, shopped at all the thrift stores and had figured out exactly what he wanted to wear; he even got a friend to help with the makeup. Finding the perfect shoes held him up a minute, but they, too, were finally discovered—at Ross, of all places.

"They have the best selection of cheap oversized shoes anywhere," he was told by that same cosmetics-providing friend as they did a test run of his face one night.

Yes, Jimmy had a surprise for everyone soon! And he could not wait ….

———◇———

Margaret Anne bustled about, hurrying to get all her morning chores and routines out of the way. She ignored

Ralph's jabs about her being too busy to be able to go anywhere and his hints and pleas to make something for him or to bring a cheesesteak back for him. Better yet, if she could come back just a little earlier so he wouldn't have to miss his regular lunch time.

She also ignored her daughter, who did not share Margaret Anne's selective style of speaking. "I'm not about to cook nothin' for that man! It wouldn't hurt him if he skipped a meal or two, you know."

A warning shot from the stern eyes of the "selectively spoken" Margaret Anne was all that was necessary on the matter of manners, back talk, and cooking for one's father.

Margaret Anne ignored her own inner voices, as well. They told her to just stay home, that the others were right. And that she really didn't deserve a day for herself.

"Oh, just shut up!" She huffed at herself as she fumbled with the comb, trying to make something of her hair as she stared in the mirror.

"Who are you telling to shut up?" Ralph yelled from the other room.

"The cat." Margaret Anne yelled back. "And you now," she said more quietly.

"What?"

"I need you for a minute. Would you get up and come in here?"

Ralph made a production of getting up from his post-breakfast nap and stepped into the bathroom. He stared briefly at his wife, who looked troubled, fumbling with something around the back of her neck. Ralph moved in behind her to help. He looked at his wife's reflection as he fastened the thin gold chain and pendant Jimmy had given her. It was that first Christmas after his first job. Ralph said, "Ya look good."

Margaret Anne looked up at him through the mirror.

Ralph shook his head and smiled. "I think you farted again."

Margaret Anne used her few words and chased Ralph from the bathroom.

<hr/>

Taking his friend's advice, Jimmy took the shoebox down from the top of his closet and placed it on the bed. He opened the box and pulled out the brand new pair of shoes he'd purchased at Ross. A size 13. A somewhat large shoe, to be sure, but Ross did indeed carry the best selection of large-sized shoes for a reasonable price. Jimmy put on a thin pair of socks and slipped his feet into the tight fitting leather. The leather— probably pleather, as the shoes were not very expensive—was also not very forgiving. He was already thankful for his friend's good advice.

"Now be sure to wear those shoes all day long and break them in before the party. And remember, you ain't just breaking in the shoes, you are breaking in them nasty feet of yours, too."

"My feet aren't nasty."

"Um, I've seen those dogs you call feet. They nasty!"

And so Jimmy spent the morning walking around his new home, putting things away, cleaning up for his mother's visit, and breaking in "them nasty feet" and his new navy blue shoes. Time flies when you waste a lot of it, and sure enough, Jimmy wasted a lot of time before finally getting himself in gear. A "wake and bake" will do that. An entire morning can pass you by and you are still mentally preparing and planning for the first task that needs to be done.

——◇——

Jimmy had just lit a candle in the combination family and dining room when he heard a knock at the door. He could hear the kitchen door rattle as the knob was twisted, and in walked his mom, Margret Anne, arms loaded with cheesesteaks, a drink carrier with two 44 ounce sweet teas, and some sticky buns for dessert. Jimmy rushed over to the door to help his mother, taking the tray of teas and the sticky buns from her, leading his mom to the square glass dining table he had inherited from his boss. Jimmy showed his mom around, explaining all the new things he had done to the two-bedroom single wide. It wasn't much, but it was his, and he was sure proud of this stepping stone on his path to more.

They sat on the couch for a bit, talking about his home, his plans for his home, and his need to hang something on the bare walls. They discussed his job and his plans for moving on and up. Jimmy was going to make something of himself. And he would, too: a strong work ethic, determination, and common sense were generally his strong suits. Margaret Ann thought his common sense might be a little off at the moment, but she ignored it and went on to complain about her husband, her other children, and the neighbors. Jimmy listened with amusement and abused them all as well. No one understood Margaret Anne quite like her youngest boy,

61

Jimmy. And no one really understood Jimmy quite like his mother, Margaret Anne. They continued their fun-filled rant at the little glass dining table over cheesesteaks and sweet teas until almost everything had been devoured.

Ralph would complain and pout if she didn't bring him something, so Margaret Anne wrapped up half of her sticky bun to take home. Then she stood to leave.

Jimmy was still engaged in his own flaky-yet-moist cinnamon delight and a cup of coffee as his mother walked around the glass table to plant a quick kiss on his forehead. And then she bid him goodbye.

"Nice shoes," she said over her shoulder, and she closed the kitchen door behind her. Jimmy looked down through the glass at the size 13 navy blue pumps with a respectable four-inch heel his nasty feet were breaking in....

"I guess I just came out to my mother," he confessed while he sat having his face painted or "beat," as the drag queen doing his makeup called it.

"She sat there that entire meal looking at them shoes through that table and didn't say a word 'til she left? Girl— she already knew."

Another older wiser friend of his offered, "They always do; they always do."

Yeah, it was gonna be one hell of a party....

Lesson 5:

———◇———

Relationships are like
an old-fashioned dance contest...
just be sure to know when your
shoulder gets tapped.

———◇———

"Fall so deeply in love with yourself that a man has to compete with YOU to get your heart."

Ms. P

"Dating as a gay man is one thing; dating as a drag queen is whole other thing."

Anna Rexia Lords

The Dance Contest

*I*t had been a long day. I was up at 4:30 AM so I could be out the door fifteen minutes later to get to the Days Inn at 5:00. The little restaurant that must have had a name—though I cannot for the life of me remember what it was—opened up at 5:30, and I was a server there. Just breakfast. Although on occasion I would stay through the lunch shift, and on an even more rare occasion, I would serve dinner. Usually at dinner time I was serving folks out past International Drive, but before you get to all that glitters in Disney... it was some seafood place that also must have had a name, but as it was doomed to fail, I fail to remember. Location and timing were the culprits along with an inability to shine.

My night serving seafood was not nearly as successful as my morning serving breakfast, but between the two I managed to pull in some good cash tips. A couple hundred bucks in the early '90s was pretty sweet! I was cut early, and rather than hitting I-4 and heading toward my eastside apartment, I took a road named after a wild fowl toward another area of town known as Metrowest. Definitely high end—at least it was then. (I have not been back in I can't remember when, but I have heard it was no longer the highly desirable neighborhood it once was. I guess that's sort of fitting given the deal I was about to make—the purchase of an 8-ball from a fellow server named something weird and trendy—Paisley, Patton, Posey—something like that.)

I pulled into a circular driveway to a fancy, newly

constructed mini-mansion. I was greeted at the door by who I guessed to be her father, a tall and rather good looking man wearing a tiny bathing suit and an open bathrobe.

"Dad! At least close your robe!" Patton or Posey or *whatever* complained.

"Oh, I'm sure your friend doesn't mind. Your father's still got it," her bikini-clad mother announced. "Would you like a drink before y'all do whatever it is you are going to do?"

"Ugh! Mother, he is just here to buy some coke." Ainsley or Ashleigh (I'm thinking now it started with an "A.") was disgusted and her tone proved it. "They are always hitting on my friends," was cast in my direction.

"Just the hot ones, dear," her dad chimed in, handing me a glass of some liquid fire; it tasted good.

As Ainsley— it was Ainsley—as Ainsley went into the back reaches of their sprawling home to grab my purchase, her parents had me on the couch between them. We took a few turns on some lines that were laid out on the coffee table before us. Ainsley returned, making another scolding comment to her folks, who were both rather close and cozy with me. We all stood and made the appropriate adjustments. My friend rolled her eyes. I handed her a wad of bills from my breakfast gig; we made our exchange and said our good-byes—a hug from my friend, a tight embrace and lingering kiss from each of her parents. As I walked out the door, I could hear Ainsley once again yelling at her parents. I got in my car and headed home, not sure exactly what I thought about that situation only because it was Ainsley's parents, but knowing what a good part of me was feeling.

After a long day, my new purchase, and a rather unexpected bump, beverage, and grope, I was excited to get home, walk in the door to a cold beer and another quick bump, a shower, and a few more lines. Then we'd see what was what.

"Hurry up and shower; they're gonna be here soon and we are gonna go!" My greeting as I walked in the door was matched with assistance in shower prep. My white uniform shirt was being unbuttoned and untucked as I was herded to the bathroom, then assisted with the removal of my remaining clothes. "Did you get it?"

"Of course," I smiled. And Randy stood on his toes and kissed me.

I knew it would always be a good evening when I came home with a good stash—or better yet, if I could surprise Randy when he got home from his job. Randy taught at a school; well, he substituted at a school, and was trying to get a job. So he always told me it was safer if I bought it. And I did. It always put me in a cleaning mood—coke did. I would vacuum like there was no tomorrow. Little rectangular imprints would form in the teal green carpet from the vacuum's suction and my Herculean effort. On a really good day, you could open the door to our third floor apartment and get knocked down by the smell of bleach, a pot of water with potpourri simmering on the stove, and knocked out by perfectly aligned teal "bricks" throughout the house. It was a magical little apartment in the Land of Oz.

By the time I showered and walked back into our room, my clothes had already been laid out on the bed—pants that fit me well and a baggy button-down shirt that brought out my eyes, apparently. I poked my head out of the bedroom to ask what was going on; I was quickly able to fill in the blanks. Mark, Tommy, and Randy had lines out on the kitchen counter, beers in hand, and they were pregaming away. Mark and Tommy were our friends from college. Mark lived with his girlfriend in a very on-again, off-again tumultuous relationship. They were always fighting or she was always nagging, or she was always going home to see her parents. But she was never around. Like ever. Which meant Mark was always with us. And if Mark was with us, Tommy was with us, because Tommy was always with Mark. He even switched schools and dropped a sports scholarship of some sort to transfer closer to his friend. Tommy wasn't particularly tall, and he was a bit on the thick side, but it was mostly that muscle over baby fat thing. He was super tan and blond. He was always around his slightly taller, slightly thinner but still muscled best friend. Tommy was also straight. Mmmhmm, oh I know, I thought the same thing ... but who was I to judge? I just made out with some chick's parents while scoring an 8-ball.

I was less concerned as to why these two straight boys were hanging out and going to a gay club with us, and more annoyed that they were already into the powder I'd purchased without at least waiting for me to get out of the shower. Not to mention that dipshit Randy had already gone through my apron and checked out my tips, and they were each using one of my hard earned twenties as straws. Killing my mood quickly.

"Um, hello...." I could see another tense evening brewing for Randy and me.

"Hey, babe!" Randy's exaggerated smile in conjunction with his thick yet well-groomed eyebrows, deeply dark Latin eyes, and those full pouty lips? I, for one, would not dare contradict. "You get one beer and one bump before we gotta go. You're the designated driver; we already started. Sorry, babe."

That smile again. He was like a hot Cuban Ernie; I was his more than willing Bert. Let me be perfectly clear, though: I did not, nor have I ever possessed a unibrow. My hair and head somewhat less cone-like. But our relationship was much the same, right down to the twin beds. Only on most nights they were pushed together.

So we headed out. I drove, as that was established while I was in the shower. Tommy had called shotgun, at least that's what Randy said.

"I did?" Tommy asked, as Randy and Mark climbed into the back of my little silver Pontiac Sunbird. It wasn't fancy, but it got me where I was going.

So Randy and Mark sat in the back, and Tommy sat by my side laughing and singing along with the music, blasting all the best from a mix-tape a friend had put together for me. It was filled with dance classics, well—hits, I guess, that would become classics. Lisa Stansfield, New Order, C + C Music Factory, Erasure. And Randy passed around lines from my earlier purchase like they were his to give. At least for him and Mark. Tommy was too busy dancing in his seat, singing at the top of his lungs, and screaming out the window. I managed to convince Randy to give me one bump at the 17/92 light. Before long, we rounded the corner of Colonial Drive and Orange Blossom Trail. There it was—the iconic red and yellow sign. Large white block letters announced the Parliament House. We had arrived.

It was truly iconic on a number of fronts: The Parliament House on Orange Blossom Trail was the last of the original Parliament House chain of motor inns, resorts, and hotels, which were often advertised as fit for the House of Lords but on a House of Commons budget. They started as a chain for families and businesses, these hotels and motels. The management of the one in Orlando was looking forward to the boom in business it would receive from the newly completed Walt Disney World Resort. But alas, International Drive and the town of Kissimmee had other hotel plans. Businesses along Orange Blossom Trail went into decline. For a brief period of time, Parliament House held significant, almost anchor store status for the now notorious Orange Blossom Trail, as OBT was known for its prostitutes and drugs and occasional sex shop.

In the late '70s, the Parliament House became known as a gay resort and night club. It continued to have its woes and successes and then more woes—even a rape and murder scandal. It had survived bankruptcy, foreclosure, recession and economic downturn, police raids, protests, and gentrification. Yet through all this, the Parliament House remained iconic. It was famous for the Footlight Players, featuring the incomparable Ms. P, forever a classic star and, for many, the soul of the Parliament House. May she rest in peace. Oh, and Ginger Minj, Courtney Act, Bianca Del Rio have all graced the stage. The Parliment House was on an upswing and on the verge of redefining itself, consistently ranking at the top of any "best of the best" lists for gay bars and entertainment venues in the United States. (There is a sad irony that the P-House managed to survive the AIDS epidemic, yet it was COVID that shut her down in late 2020.)

On this particular evening, however, it was still just a little seedy. Maybe a lot. The hotel area was a major cruising spot; folks would walk the open air hallways, hoping for a show of a different kind at an open window or perhaps an invitation to join the show with an open door. The bathrooms inside the club were a great spot for blow—the powder or the job. The drinks were strong, the music was loud, and it was always a great time on the dance floor.

We pulled into the parking area, a large gravel and dirt lot with cars lined up like they were at an old drive-in movie. We cruised through, though not in the fashion that others were cruising—we were just looking for a parking spot. We chose one near the back of the lot surrounded by a few cars, to give ourselves desired privacy. Randy pulled out my bag of white powder and offered another round. I did a hefty few lines myself.

"That's all you get for now. And only one beer and then tell them you are our DD. You get your stuff free after that." Randy mothered me.

"Water is always free and I'll probably have another beer later."

"You are driving." The smile.

"I'm also dancing, and sweating, and...I think I can drink a few beers; I'll be fine."

"But I might want a free sody-pop, and if you are a DD, you can get me one." The eyes.

Like a good Bert, I caved to the smile and Moon Pie eyes.

We headed toward the entrance and passed a few like-minded pre-gamers along the way. One couple having a fight, and another was having make-up sex or something quite hurried and quite loud in the back of a larger sedan. We got through the entrance before 10—no cover! Randy had already told me that if I made us late, I was covering the group. In fact, Randy had essentially screamed about it the whole way. We made it, and I felt like I had won $28 on a scratch-off lottery ticket and maybe a little moral high ground.

Once inside, we all split. Mark and Randy went to the drag show; Tommy blended into the crowd and appeared to be headed outside toward the pool bar; I went to the disco bar so I could grab a beer and then hit the dance floor.

The bartender and I shared a few glances; he sauntered over and asked what I needed. I told him a beer, and I bought him a shot, and then gave him my Designated Driver sob story. He winked and told me not to worry. As we were chatting away, I felt a slap on my ass. A friend of mine from school worked at the club and came by to say a special hello.

"Buy me a shot and bring me a cocktail. I'm already late!" And he rushed back behind the DJ booth, toward the backstage and dressing area for the Footlight Players.

The bartender was already pouring and putting several shot glasses filled with various liquors, a tall cocktail with an umbrella, and another beer for me on a small tray. "You're used to carrying a tray. There's a shot for each of the girls, too. Thanks, love!"

Like the professional I was, I deftly carried my tray of drinks to the dressing room. I could barely pull the curtain back to the narrow L-shaped room before I was descended upon. Squeals of "Ooh!" and "Ahh!" and "Thanks, honey!" filled the room as men of varying shapes and sizes stuffed into leggings and hose and women's undergarments grabbed at my tray and whatever else their hands could reach. An array of dresses and costumes and feather boas filled a rack while wigs and shoes and glittery bits of costume jewelry filled every shelf, table, and alcove.

I walked over to my ass-slapping friend and set his drink down. He looked at me through the mirror; large red lips and eyes painted several hues of purple stared back. "I'd say thank you, but I see you've already been well appreciated."

"You are such a bitch when you are in drag." I laughed.

"I'm not there yet. Watch this...." And he looked down as his massive hands with brightly painted nails expertly lifted what looked like a large butterfly which he delicately tore in two. A slight lift to the top left side of a deep crimson wave revealed a wicked smile. When he looked up, it was no longer my friend from that dreadful class taught by that awful man who looked just like Wilford Brimley. Staring back at me now was a glamorous, fabulous, and wildly bold version of my Nana.

"That's incredible!"

"It's all in the eyelashes. Some people think it's the hair. But they are wrong. It's the eyelashes. It's *always* the eyelashes."

"Five minutes!" An angry yell proffered by an angrier looking lesbian dressed in all black brought me back to the present. She looked like a younger goth version of a high school history teacher and softball coach. I didn't want to be reminded of school; I wanted to be exactly where I was, taking in all the sights, sounds, and stimulation of the present.

"Thank you, five!" The queens acknowledged their five-minute warning.

I took that as my cue to head back out to the disco bar. Filled with that cool white mist and the sweet plastic smell of burning fog machine fluid blended with Calvin Klein's *Eternity*, clove cigarettes, and sweat, the disco was a welcome respite from the everyday. The dance remix of "Personal

Jesus" was pounding away and my feet and white boy vogue hands, along with the rest of my invigorated body, moved out onto the floor. I'd always been a "get lost in my own world" kind of dancer. Once I heard the music, felt the rhythm, and was surrounded by bouncing and bumping and bulging shirtless men—yeah, I got totally lost in my own world. I did. I danced my heart out, I danced my aggression out, and I danced my anxiety away. When my body demanded a rest, I headed over to the bar for a glass of water, sometimes a shot with the bartender, and sometimes a cold beer. I was having a fabulous time dancing and flirting. I forgot about everything else...until I saw Tommy busting from the bathroom door and then rather abruptly bolting outside.

He looked flustered and like he wanted to disappear. So, of course I followed him. I saw him walk out past the pool to another bar next to a stage where occasionally there was live music. He went from that bar back toward the entrance and ducked into a restroom. I waited and watched the door for a minute. He never came out—so I went in. Highly reflective black tiles allowed for a near room of mirrors effect, which in turn allowed for a lot of glimpsing at potential future ex-boyfriends. But Tommy was nowhere to be seen. I interrupted a rather terse conversation between a twink of questionable age and his gentleman friend of even more questionable age and noted two other guys and some chick with big hair (not a drag queen, an actual chick) hunched over the bathroom sink, and a threesome of sorts in the stall. At least there were two sets of hands grasping the top of the stall and three sets of feet and a pair of khaki-clad knees underneath. The kneeling dude had on a pair of Weejuns minus the penny. I joined the threesome at the sink. I was offered a bump;

I accepted and I left, forgetting what brought me in there in the first place.

Back on the dance floor, Taylor Dane, Cathay Dennis, Deee-Lite, and a surprise Peter Murphy had me in my groove. After what could have been hours or what could have been minutes, drenched in sweat and smiling wide, I went back to the bar. My bartending friend hooked me up, and I took a much needed break. I was people-watching, standing against the wall with a beer in my hand when I felt an open- handed slap on the back of my head.

"Boy, how many of those have you had?!"

"What?"

"Ay que lindo, now he's deaf...."

"I'm fine, Randy. I'm drinking mostly water and dancing."

"I don't like it when you dance."

"I know." My beer is gone in one gulp and I turned toward the bar.

"Where are you going?"

"I'm getting some water. I just had a beer, and now I'm getting water."

"Ohhh get me a Sea Breeze and Mark a beer!" Those eyes and that smile.

Ohhh, but look; it's my bartender friend! I ordered the drinks: Mich Lite, Sea Breeze, and water. He stared past me as made the drinks.

"Your boyfriend is an asshole."

"I know."

"And he's fucking that friend of y'alls."

"Who, Mark? He's straight."

"Uh-huh."

"He lives with his girlfriend."

"So do I."

I laughed and asked him to sneak me a shot somehow.

"He's about as straight as that other friend of yours."

I looked over my shoulder and spotted a rather disheveled and sweaty Tommy talking with Randy and Mark. Randy made eye contact with me and snapped his fingers, pointed at Tommy, and smiled. I rolled my eyes and nodded, and turned back to the bartender who must have witnessed the exchange as he had a second beer all ready. He had an odd look on his face—a "come here," so I stepped toward him. Out of nowhere he leaned across the bar and put his mouth over mine. The gloriously warm and stinging sensation of tequila filled my mouth, along with a heavy helping of bartender tongue.

I returned with the drinks and asked how the show was. Randy and Mark filled me in on the details of the drag queens and the show, and the people they brought up on stage, and...*could I believe that for a minute they thought Mark and Randy were a thing?* But once the queens realized Mark was straight, they had to bring him up on stage. Oh, and by *all* accounts it was hilarious—I sipped my water and smiled and laughed appropriately.

Tommy had apparently been dancing; at least that's what he told Randy and Mark, which I thought was odd since I was on the dance floor the entire night, with the exception of a few side trips to see my friend behind the bar, and I hadn't seen Tommy all night. But then it hit me, I *had* seen him. Outside, when I saw him leave one bathroom and go in another. Even my bartending friend mentioned something about Tommy being a rather curious observer for a so-called straight dude. This was right after our tequila and tongue exchange. I had asked him which friend he meant. He winked.

Tommy's uncomfortable retelling of his time on the dance floor was interrupted by a loud voice over the speakers; one of the drag queens had taken over the mic and was introducing a dance contest. A Hot Summer Night Tighty Whities Dance Contest! Cheers erupted as everyone looked about for the go-go boy or bartender or bouncer who could grace us with their well-defined glory. And then the queen clarified that the contestants would be volunteers from the audience.

"Y'all check your junk now and make sure it fills them tighty whities out. We ain't just judging on how well you can Roger Rabbit! We got 'til this tired ol' queen gets her a shot and a cocktail and then we start the show! Line up there, boys," she gestured. Mama's ready to see whatcha got!"

I made a joke about how much I loved dancing. "Maybe I should join the contest."

Randy launched into a tirade, forbidding me to do it. He even evoked the bartender: "... I saw him checking you out while you were leaning against the wall with your third beer." He pronounced *against* with a long a sound, just like he always pronounced *been* with a long e. It always irritated the crap out of me.

"He just doesn't want you flaunting that dick for everyone else to see," Mark interjected. I felt like he didn't enjoy the bickering any more than I did. "He's a jealous one, you know. Completely dick-whipped."

"Really," I said, half skeptical and half hopeful.

"I don't want him to make a fool of himself," Randy spat.

"He brags about your dick more than I brag about mine," Mark laughed.

"You should totally do it, Mark!" Tommy cheered out of nowhere.

Mark blushed. Randy "oohed" and "aahed" as much as Tommy did, rallying for him to join the contest, too. Tommy said he would if Mark would. And I stood sulking about what Randy meant by me making a fool of myself all behind a smile and a forced laugh of encouragement. In a split second, away they went, Mark and Tommy, with Randy following them to make sure they signed in correctly. I grabbed another drink from the bar, was greeted with another kiss of tequila, and then I was handed a cocktail to take to the MC.

"I just got me a cocktail, and ooh it is a good one. Be sure to tip your bartenders! Next time I'm gonna have to share a tequila shot with you and your friend!" The MC thanked me with his roving eyes. "So now to the main event. Girl, mmmm, these boys and these men look so fine all dressed up!" The queen, who had clearly managed more than one shot of her own during the sign up interlude, proclaimed encouragement as she raised her cocktail in the air. "It would be a shame not to watch them take it off! Get to it, boys! Dance!"

The lights went down, the music blared, and the boys and men up on the stage now danced away, removing belts, unbuttoning shirts, and slipping out of jeans with varying degrees of success, sexiness, and—in some cases, arousal. Mark expertly and sexily managed to get his jeans down, but had trouble getting them off because of his Doc Martens. Eventually, he managed to get down to his heather gray boxer briefs. Tommy was wearing a pair of white Calvins beneath his wrinkled and worn khakis. He was not the smooth and sexy expert his buddy Mark was with regard to removing those khakis, but he did manage to kick his penniless loafers off without a fuss.

Once the dancers were down to their tighty whities or variations thereof, the elimination game would begin. Our hostess queen would tap a shoulder to send each rejected dancer away. Sometimes she would stop to engage with them, have a chat, feel their chest, touch their bottom, and then send them on their way. Sometimes she would feel them up and say, "Bring you and your well stuffed Easter Basket on over there for Round Two!" Then she'd raise her glass and ask for another, "Girl, the Lord has risen!" Randy cheered and jumped up and down when both Mark and Tommy made it to Round Two. The bartender winked from afar and indicated it was time for another shot.

The drag queen lined up the Top 10 of about 30 and then proceeded to inspect her troops. She walked up to the barely-clad young men and interviewed them one by one. Her questions were often suggestive. A crowd favorite was "If you were a bartender, how would you stir my cocktail?"

"Oh, girl! Yassss!!" rang out from a chorus of onlookers. Chest bumps, grinding, and general frivolity broke out each time the queen dropped this line. And the young men did well if they flirted in return, went along with the groping, and flaunted themselves a bit as well with some flexing and posing and teasing, lowering their waistbands to just right there. If they did not do as well, they were hit with a stinging, brutal, yet usually hilarious comment and sent backstage and away. The drag queen was narrowing the group down to what would be a Top Three dance off. Tommy was next in the line up, then Mark, and then another short dude who was really packing, and a tall guy who was more stacked than packed.

"And here is a fine, beefy stud muffin!" Tommy instantly blushed as the queen's hand fondled his beefy but firm pecs and large arms. She asked him some questions as she allowed her hand to feel his ample and meaty ass. He tightened his cheeks, flexed, and put on a real show. She touched his tight-not-toned belly; he flexed his arms and puffed up his chest some more. And then she grabbed his waistband with her drink -filled hand and plunged her other hand down the front of his briefs. With one quick tug she yelled, "And this! What kind of sweatsock has stripes? I know it ain't a Nike. It don't got no swoosh ... Next!"

Tommy bolted backstage.

Mark looked as though he had been punched in the stomach as he tried to answer the questions and do all the right things while it was his turn to be felt up and judged. He watched from the stage as his friend put his clothes back on and then disappear through a side door.

After spending some time carefully observing each of the four remaining dancers and not seeing a clear loser, the queen decided she wanted four boys to dance instead of three. Mark didn't win, but he was in the Top Four. He got a free beer for his efforts while the winner got $100. The second place prize was $50; third place prize was $25. We celebrated just the same and Randy even included me in the bump of blow as we took a pee break. One of my favorites started playing, New Order, so I said I was dancing one more song while they went to find Tommy. Four songs and another shot/kiss with the bartender and I went looking for Randy and Mark *and* Tommy. I found Tommy. He was sitting by the hotel pool all alone. I asked him if he had seen Randy or Mark.

"Maybe they are cruising the halls trying to catch some guys going at it," I joked.

"Nothing is happening over there," Tommy said, adding quickly, "They aren't over there."

"What?"

"Nothing—here they come." Tommy stood up and shot me a weird look. Then he sort of lit up, becoming animated. "Where the fuck have y'all been?"

"Looking for you, dumbass," Mark shot back.

"Take us home, boy. It's been a long day," Randy said, as he, Mark, and Tommy headed toward the parking lot.

I drove home; Randy and Mark were in the back seat again. Tommy sat—silent, beside me. He stared ahead, nodding or offering short answers when asked questions. Eventually he started quietly singing along to the music. I took that as an indication he didn't want to talk. Randy and Mark had covered up with a beach towel I had in the back. I offered to roll up the windows if they were cold, but they assured me they were fine.

We dropped Tommy off at his place. And then Mark. His girlfriend was up waiting—and audibly annoyed. Then we went back to our apartment. The beds were pushed together, though we had accomplished the task of fucking on the couch, the living room floor, the shower, and finally the balcony before we actually laid down. It had been a long day. I was angry and hurt, and I'd had a lot of tequila. Randy told me it was one of the best nights of his life when we finally laid down to fall asleep, his head on my chest and his hand firmly wrapped around the package I usually held in my own tighty whities. He snored and I stared at the ceiling. It was 4:30—time to rise and shine.

Lesson 6:

─────◆─────

There will always be bullies.
Just ask the girl who lived in the
cabin behind me.

─────◆─────

"We are looking to be accepted. We all have demons. We all have our own issues, but we all deserve love and respect."

♛

Stormy Vain

———◆———

"Boyfriends? Meh."

♛

Vicky Fischer

The Girl Who Lived In the Cabin Behind Me

*T*here is something unsettling about headlights when you glance into the rearview mirror and there they are, staring back at you. This particular time, they were accompanied by a flashing red and blue. A thing which offered a mixed bag of nerves, dread, and comfort.

<hr/>

It was my final semester of grad school at the University of Mississippi. I had just finished rehearsal for a show I was directing and was headed toward the apartment that once belonged to my dead friend Janet. It was mine now, but I still called it hers. I took over her lease after she left to pursue her PhD. When she was alive, she was Bunny—a nickname her ex-husbands and her friends from a previous life used. But I still called her Bunny, and I "played the games" as she called them. Squirrels were sqweedles, and muffins were "something we hardly ever have." She loved it when words were mispronounced or used incorrectly, like when my uncle would ask for a small piece of pie with "just a slither."

God, I wish she had met Mike, my born and bred Willards husband, whose lexicon includes "partials of land," and financial "reinversements." I believe she laughs every time I refer to her as my dead friend, Janet. And I know she is thrilled that my son "plays the games."

Bunny's was the first in a strip of four single story two-bedroom apartments. There was a little wooden cabin out back. It was in the middle of nowhere, down a road called, and I kid you not, Coon Town Road. Oh, Oxford was full of such little treasures.

On the day my father helped move me into town, we were greeted by a Confederate flag billboard declaring "Heritage Not Hate," a response to the controversy over Ole Miss having changed their logo and flag from the Confederate one to a large blue M with stars. We also saw the odd dichotomy of "The Grove," a ten-acre circle of magnolias, elms, and oaks in the heart of campus, where Ole Miss Alumni gather for the finest tailgating you could ever imagine: dining tables, fine china, chandeliers—host to the Oxford Riots and home of the Lyceum, where the bullet hole from the attempted murder of the first balck student at Ole Miss, James Meredith, can still be found.

So anyway, back to headlights: I got pulled over. I got pulled over a lot in Mississippi. I drove a little white Nissan pickup truck with Florida tags; I had long curly blond hair; and I was about as loud and, let's call it effervescent, as I am now! Oxford, being a small town in Mississippi was a place where, well, I guess I kinda stood out. And I got pulled over frequently.

Once, while on my way home from a dinner party, I was pulled over and had to take a sobriety test in a gravel parking lot. I balanced on one Birkenstocked foot as the officer shined his flashlight in my eyes and asked me all sorts of questions. My outstretched arms alternately folded in as I touched my nose while my *drunk* friend Janet hung out the window, asking the cop if she could help. The police officers were never very kind, but I was smart enough not to be doing anything else while driving.

Sometimes the headlights were not the cops, but some other patron of whatever establishment I was leaving. Sometimes they would pull up to me at the light and stare and rev the engine; sometimes it was *touch my bumper at the light* night, sometimes it was *touch my bumper as we drove*, and sometimes it was *follow me down all the roads I could imagine driving*. Like I said, there is something unsettling about headlights.

So I got home and I did not get a ticket. I got busy working on my thesis, *Equus, A Production Study*. I had battled the administration over being permitted to even do the show; there were lots of back and forth meetings with my chair, and with the Chancellor. It was even intimated that my graduation could be in jeopardy. And not for the religious objections that a production like *Equus* might pose to the conservative-minded majority in Mississippi, no. It was because there were *nekkid* people.

"Please, God help me...he's going to kill me!" and a jarring scratching at my kitchen door pulls me from my writing. And then, perhaps the most desperate and defeated cry follows—a keening wail of resignation, the low, hollow howl of hope extinguished.

It's late, maybe even pre-dawn. I open the door. Crouching before me is a bloodied and beaten young woman. I drag her in and shut the door.

A violent pounding erupts, and a male voice calls out in anger and frustration as he throws himself against the door. The girl shrieks and clings to me as we fall, backs against the door, a cacophony of animalistic growls and curses and apologies and desperate pleas to God course through it. The full length of my arms envelop the sheer panic of an animal caught in a trap while the full strength of my legs push back, holding fast against the juddering attack on my door. The pounding subsides and we can hear him, the boyfriend, cussing and screaming as he slams a car door and drives off. The headlights flash through the kitchen window, casting an eerie and momentary light over me and the bloodied girl I hold in my arms. I call the cops. She tells me a little about their fight, that he grabbed a pipe and started beating her, and somehow she got out and saw my light. . . .

It seems like an eternity, but the police arrive. We are questioned, then they go to her little cabin. They also look around my living room, these officers, one of whom has pulled me over before. They nod in my direction as he points at a picture of me in what I thought was a sweet and edgy photo—me engaged in a kiss with this guy I was dating at the time.

(Long distance, so much safer when you are in no position to ever really commit. I can't remember his name either; if pressed perhaps I could, but despite being around for some rather significant aspects of my life, he never was a key player. He was no Ray or Aaron, no Malisa or Lanna—he never really was. He did introduce me to the woman who would eventually become my ex-wife and the mother of my child. So there's that.)

The girl goes to the hospital and I do not go back to sleep. I am sure I had to teach that day. (I taught communication and acting at the University as part of my assistantship.) She moves a few days later, and withdraws from the University, I believe.

I am called to testify in court along with my friend, the police officer. The courthouse is an historic building in the middle of the town square. There are statues and plaques dedicated to the memory of those who died in service to the Confederacy. We wait outside; as witnesses, we are not allowed to watch the trial. And I remember the officer and several attractive young men dressed in their Ole Miss fraternity finest— blue blazer and khakis with a nice light blue or pink oxford and a tie. They huddle in a corner talking, smirking, and make that familiar nod in my direction. It's funny how as a gay man I am often able to be like "Ooooh, he's hot," yet recognize he would just as soon tie a rope around my neck and drag me down the street behind his daddy's BMW than give me due respect.

One by one, we are called in. I am both relieved and nervous when it's my turn to testify. I am sworn in. And I cannot help but look at the boy on trial. Maybe 20? (The age of my son right now.) I cannot, for the life of me, imagine my child beating his girlfriend with a pipe. I imagine this boy's parents couldn't either.

He is wearing his "fraternity uniform," and he just stares back at me, unafraid. I look to the girl who used to live in the cabin behind me; she looks frightened. She looks as though she would like to be anywhere else … anywhere but a few feet from the man who essentially tried to kill her. But she is here; she showed up because she wants justice for herself and legal consequences for the monster with whom she had once lived. I admire that and hope I would always take such courageous actions if and when necessary in my own life.

I give my testimony; there's something about my not stating the county and state of my address, and several "your kinds" are mentioned by the defense attorney of the "fine young man," as he is oft referred to during the trial. My testimony is rendered inadmissible. I don't understand what happened; I just know the boy gets off and the girl cries a familiar cry.

⚬————◇————⚬

I never heard from the girl again. I don't remember her parents, her mother or her father. I am sure I spoke with them. I don't even remember her name. But I remember her cries, and I remember his stare. More than anything, I remember the complete and utter defeat.

Not long after the trial, there was an evening of pounding on my windows and doors. Cries of "Are you home, faggot?" rang through the night. I kept my lights off. I sat alone on the floor in my windowless bathroom—back pressed firmly against the door. I did not call the police. Morning came. All was quiet. I looked out my window into the damp gray Mississippi morning light and stared at the quiet little cabin out back.

It wasn't long after that when I sat for my comprehensive exam. (It's a long exam, where any- and everything from the three years of study is fair game.) I sat alone, in a little room on the top floor of Bryant Hall for about 6 hours. I did have a window, with a lovely view of The Grove. I could see the Lyceum, its beautiful columns and lovely facade. And I thought about the girl who lived in the cabin behind me.

I passed my comps. I defended my thesis. I graduated with a Master's in Fine Arts in Directing in the Spring of 1997; I chose not to walk at my graduation. I convinced my parents it wasn't that important to me. The Confederate Flag was banned from Ole Miss football games the following October.

⸻◇⸻

My son, Sam, graduated high school in 2017, and he, Mike, and I took a driving vacation from Memphis to New Orleans and back again to celebrate. Sam's a huge fan of Faulkner, so Oxford and Ole Miss were on the itinerary.

We met some old friends and colleagues of mine for dinner at a little restaurant on the Square. We laughed and chatted and reminisced. And of course we all loved Bunny and spoke of her that evening. She was gone now. My friends were quick to share a story or two with Mike and Sam about my time at Ole Miss. Of course there were the shows, and my directing. Theatre was a brilliant escape. There was a baffling, but flattering comment made about me making a difference for LGBTQs in the Ole Miss and Oxford communities. And while I'd love to believe that is true, I just remember trying to be me, trying to figure out who that was, and trying to do it without getting beat up or killed.

We wandered the streets of Oxford, Faulkner's home, the Ole Miss campus, the Lyceum and its famed bullet hole; there is now a James Meredith memorial. Upon wandering into Off-Square Books, where I once directed a stylized and bluesy version of Harold Pinter's *The Lover*, we saw their shirts for Pride Week. Oxford, Mississippi had a Pride Week!

I don't know when I'll get back to Oxford, if ever, although I'd like to. And not to be too philosophical, but you can't ever really go back, can you? The Oxford I shared with Sam and Mike? That was not my Oxford, not my memory.

91

Neither were a lot of what my friends had to share. My memories are different, scattered, yet from a time that may have been one of the most formative in who I would become. And while I am beyond thrilled that the progressive little town of Oxford is trying to shine some light in what is still a rather hostile environment for folks like me, there is a bizarre and selfish loss within me—of a time I worked so hard to forget. Of moments and fears and hardships I worked so hard to bury. It's as though the town had also put those things away, into a little compartment, deep in its own personal memories of its own history, and that they no longer matter. Only they do.

———◇———

It is odd, twenty-something years later to share that story, here, in Salisbury— a town that's getting ready to host its first Pride Week. To share that story where, once again, I had to learn who I was and come out all over again—primarily to myself. To learn to be a father and a husband. And my hair, while not long and flowing, is something I'd like to think my dead friend Janet would still call *stylish and attractive*. I am just as loud and effervescent as I was during my time in Mississippi, but I've never had the same fears or worries here as I did when I was in Oxford. I'm smarter; well, that's debatable, but I'm more seasoned, battle-scarred. And mostly, I am just more aware. And Salisbury is a different town, in a different place.

The glare of headlights can still haunt me, though it has to do more with my age and my corresponding terrible eyesight. The glare, the scattered light, make it difficult to see clearly. Generally that is more head on. When the lights come from behind, I've finally learned to flip that little tab on the rearview mirror, and the lights are no longer in my eyes. We don't get that little tab with memories, do we?

I wonder about that girl, though. The girl who lived in the cabin behind me. Did it break her? That time when justice failed. That day when the man who invited her into safety was a "your kind" and the man who beat her was "a fine young man." I wonder if she had the resolve to overcome what happened to her that day down Coon Town Road, in Lafayette County, just outside of Oxford, Mississippi. I wonder if she went back. I wonder if she was told she made a difference. I wonder if she knows what an impact she had. And I wonder if she knows what a hero she is ... to me.

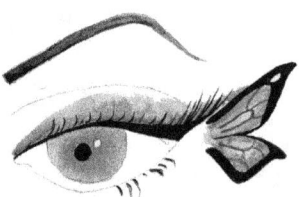

Lesson 7:

In times of grief or struggle,
we must rise and celebrate
who we are ... in the name.

"I don't know what to tell you, darlin'.
If you don't like it that way, change it."

♛

Mama ChaCha

In the Name

*I*t was as though a hospital and a hotel efficiency got together and had a love child, this child—this suite of rooms where Mama ChaCha lay. She was surrounded by her children. The folds of her hospital gown spilled out from her, and constantly had to be readjusted; the blue-green cotton blend, its nondescript pattern and ties and buttons in all the wrong places. She would tug at it or pull. On better mornings she would wave her arms as she danced in her mind. Adorned, they were, with a simple wrist watch, a homemade friendship bracelet, and her medical wristband. Now they were tucked neatly under her sheets and blankets. Atop her head was a crown of knit fabric, a green and yellow and red and black toboggan with a friendly nod to Bob Marley; the herbs he would often enjoy somehow woven in. She didn't pick it, goodness no; it was a hasty grab from a convenience store purchased on the drive to see her on some visit or another—and it only cost $10. But it did the job; it kept her head warm. She looked about the room with love for her children. They weren't hers, of course, yet they were. Like a mother goose, at some point she had taken each of them under her wing, honking instructions and cautions and love.

And the room. That union of medical convenience and family comfort was a welcome change from the sterile and public nature of a shared room at a nursing facility that had long since passed its own prime. Pictures of Mama ChaCha with her children were placed on every tabletop and surface available. The beige yet gray draperies filled the windows but were kept open to allow for a little bit of natural light, though the days were gloomy and dark. A large fluorescent strip overhead offered a stark white glaring sense of reality, while the small table lamp from home offered a more comforting amber glow. These were all off now; even the soft silver of sunlight on a cold and rainy February day had turned purple, blue, and black—still dappled with rain.

She called softly, "Glass." That is as much as she could say, though we all knew what she meant. Mama ChaCha needed her eyeglasses. She pulled her arms from beneath the folds of her blankets, waving them about and singing along with Gloria Gaynor. "I Will Survive" was playing softly on a borrowed CD player. It was an impressive show, as most of the time now she would just rest. Her lips had lost most of their color, and her eyes were wide and dark and hollow. The yellow of her cheeks added an unmistakable understanding as to where she was in life's cycle now. She struggled to adjust the frames of her glasses; finally choosing to hold them as if she were at the opera. Mama ChaCha looked about the room, straining to focus on her children.

"I see Missy and I see Andy." She wore a wide smile as she peered through her glasses. "I see Timmy and— is that Anita? I love you!"

So many people gathered those final days. Mama ChaCha's suite of rooms became a bustling center of activity as the many facets of her incredibly, supremely, seriously, monumentally compartmentalized world came together. It was, all at once, all the lives Mama ChaCha had ever lived. It was the return line at Walmart after Christmas. It was the long drives taken to Federalsburg and Rehoboth and Wimington and Bush River. It was the card games and the drag shows and the deep dark secrets and shadows and memories and regrets. It was the people she had cared for and the people who had cared for her. It was the park-and-ride and the picnic tables. And it was home.

We sat with Mama ChaCha one night—four of us did—and it was cold. The rain was struggling to become something softer, something brighter, something like snow—but the snow never came. We played cards, as we always did, and shared memories and stories and little life lessons from Mama ChaCha. We laughed and we cried, and we knew we all needed to go home. Mama ChaCha was tired. She needed to go to sleep.

<hr>

It was just before 5 a.m. The darkness and the rain still lingered, as Mama ChaCha's children all slept in their beds like good little girls and boys should. But that was when I heard it—Mama ChaCha's voice. I opened my eyes; I looked out the window and saw ... snow.

It was just after 5 when we got the call. Mama ChaCha had passed away in her sleep.

<hr>

While I will always cherish those last moments with Mama ChaCha, they sometimes haunt me. The sad times are never how we want to be remembered. It's not how she would have wanted to be remembered. "I don't know what to tell you, darlin'. If you don't like it that way, change it." I can hear her say. "Bless your heart, you always gotta make it so hard."

So I changed it.

It was as if a unicorn farted and shat out *Romper Room.* Mama ChaCha was surrounded by her children. The folds of her gown spilled out over her bed like some vibrant waterfall—a cascade of chiffon and satin. Delicate lace and tiny pearls and beads and sequins gave her the appearance of a QVC wedding cake, decked out in some of the finest bedazzling any good southern church lady could imagine. Her tiara, no—it was her crown, and it shone brightly. And she looked about the room with love at her adoring children.

And the room! That unicorn shart of glitter and rainbows was a welcoming and wondrous world to her children. Pictures of Mama ChaCha with her children adorned every tabletop and surface available. Draperies of every color swagged about the windows, while tapestries with woven stories and memories and wisdom hung from the walls. A large glittering chandelier that looked to us as though it could have been made from diamonds, sapphires, and rubies filled the room with a magical glow. Strings of pearls and crystal draped from the golden and jeweled arms which held the soft warm light.

And there was another light; not from the glitterball brilliant chandelier, and not from the magnificently bejeweled crown that rested atop her head. No, this light simply emanated from her very soul. Brilliant, warm, and welcoming. Oh, and then she lifted her magic mirror from the deep folds within her gown and smiled. She pulled a black tube from beneath her décolletage, corseted as she was it was an impressive show. She added to the deep burgundy red of her lips, and opened her painted eyes wide—her eyelashes iridescent wings of a butterfly. The rouge on her cheeks added luster and dimension to her oval face, lifting her cheeks, and offering edges. She moved the mirror forward, as though she was no longer looking into it, but through it. And she was ... to see us!

And we sat enthralled, every one! Looking up at her, looking up to her, wondering, anticipating, trembling on the very brink of hope—who would she see? What would she say? And what would we learn today? We all sat crisscross applesauce, hands in our laps, as proper young pupils should. We giggled with excitement and joy, and just a little bit of jealousy with every name called. And when it was *our* turn, when we heard *our* name, when she looked through that magic mirror and it was *our* face she saw and it was *our* name she called...!

"I see Missy and I see Andy." She smiled wide as she peered through her glass and called us lucky ones by name. "I see Timmy and Anita and Camile and little Sammy, too. I see all of my children, and children...I love you!"

In Case You Need It

The Trevor Project
(866) 488 7386
www.thetrevorproject.org

LGBT National Youth Hotline
(800) 246 7743
www.glbthotline.org

LGBT National Hotline
(888) 843 4564
www.glbthotline.org

True Colors United
(212) 461 4401
www.truecolorsunited.org

PFLAG National
(202) 467 8180
www.pflag.org

PFLAG Salisbury
www.salisburypflag.com

About the Author

Andrew Heller received his MFA in Directing from the University of Mississippi and his BA in Theatre from the University of Central Florida. A Florida native, he now resides on Maryland's Eastern Shore. He has worked as a director, an Equity stage manager, and an educator from pre-k through college. He is the Senior Publishing Consultant for Salt Water Media in Berlin, Maryland. Andrew has published the Samuel Smythe young adult adventure series as well as a book of plays titled *A Bunch of Ellipses.* This is his fifth book.

"Oh, get the hell over it!"

Mama ChaCha